PRELUDE TO A SHOWDOWN!

The rhythms of Russ's breathing subtly changed, increasing slightly. Then the volume faded and Caloon could no longer hear it. He knew with certainty that Russ was awake, that somehow, even though alseep, he had received a signal of danger and was now roused and alert.

Barely audible, muffled by Russ's blankets and probably also by his hand, Caloon heard the click of the six-gun being cocked. Caloon smiled and nodded in the blackness. With his keen reflexes Russ might survive for a short time in the dangerous world. Maybe just for a little while. . . .

Nighthawk

F. M. PARKER

FAWCETT GOLD MEDAL · NEW YORK

The Making of the Land—
A Prologue

Only the hot eye of the primeval sun saw the birth. Watched the water womb of the ocean torn aside and the breast of a new continent rise to life upon the earth. This earliest dawning of the land took millions of years, but only a minute of time in the unimaginably long life of the world.

Propelled by some irresistible energy within the bowels of the earth, the continent battled to emerge, crowding away the salty brine of the sea. Exposed for the first time to the brilliant light of the day were massive layers of sandstone, limestone, and shale piled thousands of feet thick by the energetic waters of the sea. During the passage of a few more million years, the broad land plain grew a fertile cover of soil and came alive with countless species of life.

A great mountain range with scores of tall peaks lay to the north of the plain. The mountain's crest cut crosswise the path of the prevailing storms that drove in from the west, forcing the moisture-laden air to rise abruptly. And the sky-brushing crown of the mountain milked the clouds, wringing billions upon billions of gallons of water from them to fall upon the land.

The water rushed down from the rocky crags of the mountains, collected into rivulets, which grew into creeks that merged to form a mighty river. Lesser streams were born on the plain itself. Some of them hurried off to find the sea. Most found the mighty river from the north and added their volume to its prodigious flood.

For countless thousands of years the great river meandered back and forth across the plain, cutting into the land, carving a wide valley to carry its never ending flow. And the millennium passed, score after score, adding to millions of years.

During this long span of time, gigantic pressure again built up in the crust of the earth. The awesome might, too powerful to be contained, began to lift and arch the plain.

The change in the slope of the land altered the gradient of the streams, forcing them from their channels, destroying them. All except one, that is, the giant river from the north. The source of its water, the mountains, were also rising and their increased height squeezed ever more moisture out of the clouds. This enlarged volume of water and the steepening of the grade charged the river with new vigor and energy. It now moved more swiftly and carried vast quantities of sand and gravel.

Using its torrent of water as a blade and the abrasive sand and gravel as the teeth of that blade, the river sawed at the bottom of its channel, fighting to retain its familiar bed. At times it almost lost, forced within inches to abandon its course. In the end it won, but it was a strange-appearing river; though it had long looping meanders of old age, it flowed swiftly with the lustiness of youth.

The forced upward bowing of the land had created great tension upon the rock layers. One added inch of movement exceeded the strength of the rock and faults of unbounded force sliced up through the earth's crust. Vents and fissures gaped open at the surface. The zones of weakness along the fault zones reached deep within the earth, tapping into the live core of the planet and allowing boiling, molten rock to gush out.

Red-hot and charged with volatile gasses, the liquid rock flowed down the slightest incline, smothering square mile after square mile with a blanket of death. As the lava surged across the ancient landscape, it trapped the panicked animals, burning them to ashes in a moment, and incinerated the grasses and weeds into a thin carbon film.

Sometimes the outpourings slowed and even stopped, and at other times burst forth with great violence, blowing ash thousands of degrees hot upon the land. One lava flow piled upon another. After many eruptions over hundreds of centuries, hard rock more than two miles thick was formed.

This cataclysmic upheaval of the land threatened the river. Faults slashed across its course and lava poured into its channel. But again the river beat back its attackers. As the walls of the faults rose to bar its passage, the mighty torrent pounded great gaps through them. And the cold mountain water of the stream solidified the liquid lava into massive blocks, then ground those chunks of dead rock into sand and flushed it away to the ocean.

Finally the stress on the stone foundation of the plain slackened and faded away. The lava cauldrons deep within the earth were again capped off. The land rested. The rains fell.

The river and lesser streams continued to devour the land as they had since time immemorial. One stream was especially aggressive, the one that stemmed from the direction of the morning sun. It cut headward, breeching the channels of smaller currents and consuming their floods. It could not rival the north river, however, and paid homage by bestowing its total flow upon that ancient stream.

The voracious appetite of all the many currents wore away the ash and softer lava beds, leaving the superhard cores of the volcanic eruptions standing as young, angular mountains surrounded by wide flat valleys.

The climate turned dry, a desert grew, and its desiccating winds ravaged the country. The streams that had once run all year now had only short seasons of life in the sun, flowing in their courses only small fractions of their lengths before the thick sand and gravel of the valley bottoms swallowed them hungrily.

Some of the animal and plant species adapted to the harsh land of desert valleys and mountains. Other species died.

That is the way man found the land.

Chapter 1

Arizona Territory—February 1884

The winter storm, howling like a she-wolf that has lost her pup, rushed down from the arctic. Powerful gusts of wind buffeted the stone walls of the ranch house built on the bluff above the valley. The hammer blows of the wind rattled the window pane where John Blackaby stood looking out.

Blackaby reached out a calloused old hand and pressed the glass tightly into its sash to stop the noise. He shivered at the touch of the frigid glass. Getting old, he thought. I can't stand the cold like I used to. He was glad for the flames that crackled in the fireplace behind him.

Wind-driven curtains of snow scurried away to the south, hiding the valley from Blackaby's view beyond a few hundred yards. From the bunkhouse smoke rose, to be snatched away and shredded by the wind almost before it could climb out of the chimney.

To the right of the bunkhouse, the large stone corrals lay empty. All the horses and the dozen or so sick range cows that had been brought into headquarters for doctoring were in the stables, snugly hidden from the storm.

The nearest snow squall, torn suddenly by an erratic shift in the wind, split into many ribbons. The streamers of snow poured down like miniature waterfalls to bury the desert in white. And they pelted with stinging blows the three horsemen that pushed in from the east.

Blackaby spotted the dark forms of the men and walked to where his holstered six-gun hung on a wooden peg beside the fireplace. "Three riders coming," he said to his wife as he buckled the gun to his waist.

Sarah Blackaby rose from her chair near the fire and followed him to the window. "The weather isn't fit for people to be traveling in," she said.

"Maybe they got caught by the storm," answered Blackaby, "or have some other game to play. Anyway, we'll soon know, for they're coming straight in."

Dan Tamblin raised his head and squinted into the stinging ice pellets. Through a break in the storm, he saw the ranch house, a large two-story structure with its lava rock walls showing black against the snow-covered land.

He turned to see if his father and daughter had seen the house. They rode with their heads tilted down so the brims of their hats protected their faces. Snow was piled on the shoulders of their heavy sheepskin coats. Not once had they complained during the long cold trip from Tucson. He was proud of both of them.

"Less than a quarter mile to go," he called.

Both lifted their heads to stare ahead. "Damn big house," said Lafe Tamblin. "The owner must be prospering to afford it. Sam, do you see how big it is?"

"I see it, Grandfather. It is large. Looks out of place here in the desert. Do you think this Mr. Blackaby will be agreeable to our plan?"

"We'll soon know," answered Lafe.

The Tamblins rode directly up to the hitching rail at the main house and dismounted. "Wait here and stay away from the ranch hands," said Dan. He separated from the others and climbed the flight of stone steps leading up to the house.

The ranch foreman had seen the three horsemen arrive, and now he and two ranch hands left the warmth of their fire and came outside. While the foreman continued toward the house, the other men pulled their heads down into the collars of their coats and stood with rifles in the crooks of their arms and watched the strange riders.

Dan Tamblin noted the men with the rifles taking position near the bunkhouse and a third man hurrying up the grade toward him. The defensive actions of the ranch crew were easily understood; three unknown horsemen coming in out of the storm could likely as not mean trouble.

At Dan's knock, an old man with thin gray hair opened the door. With his hand on his six-gun, he measured the stranger with hard eyes. Finally he said, "Come in out of the weather."

"Thank you," said Dan. He removed his hat, slapped it against his leg to send a shower of icy snow flying, and stepped inside.

"My name is Tamblin, Dan Tamblin," he said as he stripped off his glove and shoved out a hand.

"John Blackaby is my name," said the rancher, taking the proffered hand, feeling the thick calluses on the palm. "Come over by the fire and warm yourself. It's cold outside so tell your friends to come in too, if you want."

"They're all right outside," said Tamblin, moving up to the fireplace and turning his back to the flames.

The old woman remained near the window and watched the two figures, bundled in their heavy coats, walk back and forth along the hitch rail. One stood almost a head taller than the second. Now and then the smaller would turn his head and say something. The second made only very brief answers and often turned to observe the men with their rifles at the bunkhouse.

"Bad storm we're having, so you must have a mighty good reason for being out," said Blackaby.

"Yes, it's a mite rough, but we've been in worse. I do have something important I want to talk with you about."

"What would that be?"

"Running cattle in the Growler Mountains," responded Tamblin, watching the old man's face.

"Well, there's free government range over there in the Growlers and all the other mountains to the west of us. But there's a complication—that's rustler range."

"I've heard the tales," said Tamblin, "but I expect they are exaggerated like most such stories are."

"Not stretched at all," snorted Blackaby. "They're all true as hell. They'll have you robbed blind before the summer is over. They take some of my cows every year and I have twenty riders. How many cowboys do you have?"

Before Dan could answer, the outside door opened and the foreman came in without knocking. He crossed the room to stand beside Blackaby.

"This is Harry Tullos," said Blackaby. "Best, and, I might add, the toughest ranch honcho in a hundred miles, any direction. Meet Tamblin. Wants to run cattle in the Growlers."

"Howdy," said Tullos, making no effort to shake hands. "That's been tried once before by a fellow. We found his bones bleaching out on the desert. Rustlers must of found him right off cause he didn't even have time to build a cabin. His cows were all gone, too."

Tamblin decided to change the subject from talk of the rustlers. "I made an inspection trip through the Growlers and found good grass on the higher slopes, especially the north and east ones."

Blackaby nodded. "I agree there's grass. That ain't the problem. You can't keep cattle. They just up and go south to Mexico."

Tamblin was tired of this kind of talk. "Well, my cows go only in the direction I want. And since the rustlers are such a bother, you won't have any objections to me running a herd on the mountain. My place would act as a buffer between your stock and the rustlers."

"All men are allowed to make mistakes and I think going to the Growlers would be one," said Blackaby. "After the Army finally gets out here and hangs the rustlers, things will be better. As far as your ranch being a buffer between my cattle and the rustlers, I doubt they would be much benefit. Why do you ask me if you can run cows over there?"

"Your spread is the nearest ranch to the Growlers, probably not much over twenty miles or so east. I need to know where your west line is. I don't want my cows eating your grass."

"I appreciate that. Ajo Mountain is part of my range. Let's say the base of the west face of the mountain will be the dividing line separating your range and mine."

Tamblin knew Blackaby lied and was claiming at least ten thousand acres more than he used. The Double B–branded cattle did not get farther west than the lower eastern slopes of Ajo Mountain. Dan had carefully noted that fact the past autumn when he had ridden over Ajo Mountain going to the Growlers.

"Your cattle don't get past the top of Ajo. But I agree with the boundary. Any cattle I find of yours, I will shove back to the mountain. Any you see with my brand, just haze west down in the valley."

"All right," said Blackaby. "Where's your herd now?"

"About five miles east of here."

Blackaby looked at him sharply, and his eyes hardened. "Well, I see you planned to go to the Growlers despite what I said. And I can see you don't believe what we say about the rustlers. But have you considered that because of this extra cold winter, green grass will be a couple of months late?"

"Yes, I've thought of that, but I want to get an early start. I plan to turn my stock out on last year's old grass until the new green-up comes."

Sarah Blackaby interrupted, speaking from the window. "The Growlers are not a fit place for that young woman. She'll not be safe there."

"There are no women in my family," said Dan, beginning to button his coat. "Just my father and my son, Sam."

Mrs. Blackaby had been studying the smaller person outside, had noted the hand gestures, the manner of walk, the way the head was held, and knew with complete certainty it was a female. Sarah's wise old eyes caught Tamblin's look, saw the controlled, noncommittal expression on his face. She understood he wanted no person to know there would be a woman in that isolated, bandit-infested land.

"Your son may want to talk to someone other than his dad and grandfather. If that happens, ask him to come visiting. It's only a short day's ride and I could use some company myself."

Tamblin read the woman's measuring stare, and concluded she was on to his strategy. He hoped she would not give it away. "I will tell him of your kind invitation. I'll say good-bye now." He touched his forehead in greeting to the woman and crossed the room to the door in long strides.

Samantha Tamblin saw her father emerge from the house and hurry down toward them. She watched his progress, waiting expectantly.

"How did it go, Dad?" she asked eagerly. "Any objections from Blackaby?"

"Everything went fine as far as reaching an agreement on who had what range. But the rustler stories appear to have more truth in them than we thought. Sam, it may not be safe for you and we had better find a place for you to stay in Tucson."

Sam stepped close to her father and put her hand on his arm. "Please don't be afraid for me. I'll always stay near you or Grandfather. That way I'll be safe." She squeezed his arm and turned her smiling face to include the elder Tamblin. These two men were her happiness, her very life. They wanted a ranch of their own, had worked many long years to accumulate the cattle to start it. Nothing must stand in the way of reaching that goal. Least of all her.

"After we have become very prosperous, maybe even rich, I will travel to St. Joseph and go to a proper young ladies' school. And to do it all very correctly, I'll spend a lot of your and Grandfather's money to buy beautiful clothes to fill a whole room."

She stepped to her horse, brushed the accumulation of snow from the seat of the saddle with her gloved hand, and swung astride. "Let's go. We'll growl right back at the Growler Mountains. No Tamblin is a coward." She reined the horse away from the hitch rail and out of the yard.

Dan Tamblin looked at his father. "She must never be out of our sight. And by God we will raise a lot of cows in two years, or maybe three; we'll have enough money to see that she goes to St. Jo in style."

Lafe Tamblin's hand touched the butt of his six-gun. "Maybe I'm a little old, and I'm not as fast as I once was, but I'm still pretty damn good with this. And I'd fight Satan himself to keep her out of danger. She can have all my share of the money we make anytime she needs it."

They mounted and spurred to catch the girl.

Sarah left the window and reseated herself near the fire.

"They'll not last a year," prophesied Blackaby. "Either

renegade Indians or the outlaws will kill them. Unless they pack up and get out of that country."

"I do not believe they will leave by their own free will," said Sarah.

"Then they are all dead people," declared Blackaby.

Chapter 2

Arizona Territory—March 1884

Jacob S. Kempt, superintendent of Yuma Territorial Prison, arose before daylight and dressed quickly in the dark. He left his residence on the bluff above the Colorado River and climbed the gravelly road leading up the steep slope of Prison Hill.

Kempt glanced up at the top of the hill where the tall black silhouette of the prison walls obscured the brittle brightness of the desert stars. Then he swung his look down at the sleeping town of Yuma. The safety of all those people and the several hundreds more scattered across the Arizona desert was his responsibility. It was a heavy load. Reinforced in his determination to carry out his plan, he hurried up the grade.

At the iron-barred gate of the north sally port, he called out loudly. "Guard on duty, this is Superintendent Kempt. Open up."

A guard carrying an oil lantern and a Winchester rifle came out of the guard shack and hurried the few feet to the gate. He lifted up the light so its rays would shine between the heavy bars and illuminate the face of the man standing in the darkness just outside.

"Good morning, Mr. Kempt," said the man. He set the lantern down and pulled the thick locking bolt free from its embedded slot in the four-foot-thick adobe-and-stone wall. The gate swung open easily on its greased hinges.

"Hello, Pike," said the superintendent, stepping through the entryway that was dwarfed by the massive wall. "Is everything in order this morning?"

"Yes, sir. The prisoners have been up and getting ready for over an hour."

"Good," said Superintendent Kempt. He led the way back into the guard shack. "Light another lantern and hand it up to me." He continued across the room and began to climb a stout wooden ladder bolted to the wall. Upon reaching the ceiling, he unlocked a heavy trapdoor, and hauled himself through it to step out upon the three-foot-wide top of the exterior prison wall.

"I'll be in the west gun tower for an hour or so," Kempt called down to Pike.

"Yes, sir," answered the guard. "Here's your lantern."

Kempt lowered the trapdoor and heard Pike ram the bolt home to lock the passageway. The strict adherence to security rules pleased the superintendent. He held the lantern out before him and moved off cautiously along the narrow catwalk.

A second guard on duty in the gun tower saw Kempt approaching and unlocked the entrance. He remained near the opening, holding his rifle ready, waiting for the superintendent to come inside to safety.

"Good morning, Mr. Kempt," said the guard.

"Good morning, Teller," responded Kempt. "I'll be out on the landing until the prisoners leave."

"Anything you need from me, sir?" asked the guard.

"No. You may go back to your station," said Kempt and crossed the small room and went out onto the narrow balcony fronting the tower.

The wind gusted in cold from the snow on the mountains to the north. Chilled, the superintendent put his hands into his pockets and, his brow furrowed with misgivings, stood looking out across the dark prison yard.

Kempt allowed his ears and eyes to range out across the yard and buildings. He believed a penitentiary had a life, a character of its own, and the actions of its inmates were its pulse. He felt confident that from watching and listening to the prisoners in the exercise court, or in the chow line, he could detect when a breakout attempt was brewing, or judge how near a riot was to exploding. At least he had been successful in reading such signs for the past twenty years, and had not once lost control of his savage charges.

And he judged that within the next two or three days, all hell would break loose—unless he moved now, decisively, ruthlessly.

In the middle of February, the territorial governor had informed the superintendent that the U.S. Congress had again approved the Arizona Territory budget without funding his request for enlarging the penitentiary. That had left Kempt with an intolerable situation.

Expanded twice since its original construction in 1876, the prison was designed to hold forty-two prisoners. It now held one hundred and six murderers, bank robbers, and other felons. Eight prisoners were crowded behind the bars of each nine-foot-by-eight-foot cell. The only furnishings in the cubicles, which were carved into the live rock of the hill, were two tiers of bunks three beds high. Two convicts had to sleep on straw pallets on the floor, their faces within inches of the stinking slop buckets full of human waste.

Fights among the inmates in the cramped quarters were daily occurrences. Three of the most severely injured men were in the infirmary, one with a cracked skull and two with knife wounds.

By the end of February, Kempt had devised a plan that might, with a great amount of good luck, get him safely through the year until the next Congress met. He would construct a temporary prison with convict labor. Build it far out in the inhospitable desert, miles from water, and encircle it with a tall stone wall. Once it was finished, he would use the inmates locked up there to quarry and haul to Yuma the stone that would be needed to expand the main prison when funding was provided.

Carefully he had selected thirty-two halfway manageable inmates, taking great pains to pick men whose absence would break up the cliques and gangs that existed within the prison. He had considered sending just the trustees and those inmates with short sentences remaining. But he needed those men at the main prison; several of them were his spies, his indispensable eyes and ears inside the walls.

He chose six of the toughest guards to go with the prisoners. For added insurance, two Quechan Indian trackers were hired at a monthly salary of thirty dollars each. Kempt also promised them fifty dollars in gold as a bounty for the return, dead or alive, of any prisoner who tried to escape.

The first gray light of dawn crept over the tall white-washed walls and Kempt began to make out the forms of the other buildings inside the compound. There was a light in the mess hall, but he knew the inmates that were leaving today would already have eaten. Lights also shined from the barred windows of the main cell block. Now and then he caught the sound of a distant complaining voice.

The sun, still hidden below the horizon, speared a high feathery cloud in the eastern sky, coloring it dark red like a smear of blood. Kempt raised his view to look outside the prison at the sunrise. Then dropped his eyes to glance up the valley of the Gila. He found the river meandering sluggishly toward him, its water a wet silvery sheen in the growing light.

Beneath the bluff on the north side of the prison, the Gila was swallowed by the mighty Colorado River, surging in swollen with snow-melted water from the Rocky Mountains. Then the waters of the two rivers, joining in a great flood, rushed south in search of the salty waters of the Gulf of California.

A steamboat whistle broke the morning stillness and Kempt knew the captain of the large stern paddle-wheel vessel that had arrived the day before was preparing to cast off on his return journey downriver. After a two-day run down to the Colorado, the boat would find the calm blue water of the Gulf of California. There the shallow-draft river craft would wait for the sleek clipper sailing ships that came hurrying down the California Coast from San Francisco with their tons of supplies. The cargo would be off-loaded onto the riverboat and ferried up the river to Yuma and the penitentiary. The puffing boats with their bales and boxes of supplies, and bronze steam whistles tooting, were always a welcome sight to the isolated townsfolk.

The jingle of chain and stamp of horse hooves sounding from the compound drew Kempt's attention back inside. He saw four guards, each leading a team of horses, come out of the stables.

Calling orders to the animals in low voices, the men positioned them astride the tongues of wagons heavily laden with grain for the horses, food and tools for the men, and iron bars and doors for the new prison. The guards hooked the traces of the harness to the wagons, climbed up into the high seats, and picked up the reins.

The door of the main cell block swung open. A guard wearing sergeant's stripes came out, moved away a few paces, and stood ready with his Winchester. "Bring them out," he ordered in a loud voice.

Four men, at spaced intervals fastened by wrist manacles to lengths of chain, shuffled out, moved away from the door, and stood clumped together. Another bunch came out, and yet another, until there were eight knots of men in the yard.

Several prisoners, knowing Kempt often spied on them from the gun tower, sullenly looked in his direction. Even at this distance, Kempt felt their hating eyes on him.

A second guard came through the open door from the cell block and called to the sergeant. "All's ready."

"Two strings of prisoners go to the rear of each wagon," commanded the sergeant.

The prisoners strung themselves out in rows and moved toward the wagons. As each group reached a wagon, the second guard fastened the end of their chain to steel locks bolted to the rear of the vehicles.

"That sure as hell will hold you," said the guard. He turned and called to the man with the rifle. "They're chained."

The sergeant nodded his head and hurried across the prison yard to the gun tower. He looked up at the man on the landing and saluted.

"Mr. Kempt, the prisoners are ready to leave."

"Very good, Sergeant," acknowledged the superintendent. "Make reports of your progress every third day. Work the ass off the prisoners and they will give less trouble. I don't want any of them to escape. Is that fully understood?"

"Yes, sir," answered the guard.

"Send Gray Antelope to me," directed Kempt.

"Yes, sir." The guard saluted, about-faced, and hastened to join the cavalcade of men and wagons forming up in front of the north gate.

Kemp watched the procession file out through the

opening in the great wall. From habit he counted the prisoners as they were towed along behind the wagon.

The prisoners' odds for making good an escape attempt increased greatly once they were outside the walls. If by some bad fortune he was to allow these thirty-two criminals to get loose on the people of the territory, his professional career was finished. But he knew there was no alternative to his plan.

A remuda of seven spare horses herded by the Quechan Indians on horseback trotted clattering up the caliche bank from the meadows along the Colorado River. They fell in at the rear of the column. The sergeant called out to the Indians and one turned his mount and rode into the prison and up beneath the gun tower. He looked up at Kempt without uttering a sound.

"Gray Antelope, hear me clearly," said the superintendent, leaning over the railing of the balcony and speaking in a hard voice. "If any prisoner tries to escape, bring him back dead. Do you savvy? Dead!"

"Savvy," said the Indian, his large black eyes staring back without emotion from under the prominent ridges of his brow. He spun his pony and spurred it from the prison yard. Inside his mind he smiled. He would make many gold coins during the next year.

Chapter 3

The cackling laughter of the crazy prisoner drifted across the sun-baked prison compound. In the shade of the porch of the commissary, a guard unpropped his chair from against the wall and looked at the man. Why didn't the lunatic keep his mouth shut and stop that infernal crowing?

"Crazy, you'll have a heat stroke out there in the sun," the guard yelled at the tall, lanky man laying the stone wall of a new building in the hot August sun.

"No, sir, not me, Guard Al," answered Crazy Caloon, raising his head to stare at the man with the rifle. "I just want to be sure to finish this guardhouse so you and the other guards will have a warm place come winter."

With a horny finger, Caloon flicked away a rivulet of sweat from the beads on his forehead and the puddles in his sun-bleached eyebrows. He finished wiping his face with the sleeve of his worn prison shirt and reached for another piece of lava rock.

"Hell, man, it's three months before it'll turn cold," called the guard. "Go on inside and loaf like the other prisoners 'til it cools off. It must be a hundred and twenty degrees in the shade.''

Crazy Caloon skillfully finished fitting the slab of stone onto the straight, plumb wall and then looked searchingly at the guard. "Are you telling me I can't work anymore?" he asked dejectedly, and cocked his head to the side and watched the guard.

"No, I'm not saying that," said the man, his voice climbing a notch in anger. He could catch a couple winks of sleep if the prisoner would go into his cell and settle down. "Kill yourself if you want to. I'm saying you can get into the shade until the sun drops a little lower if you want."

"Thank you, Guard Al, but working will make my twenty years go faster." Caloon laughed again, shrill as the excited chatter of a squirrel.

"Okay, have it that way," said Al. Best let the man alone; the sergeant would raise hell if he caught a guard trying to get a prisoner to stop working, no matter how hot it was. He repropped his chair against the wall and closed his eyes.

Crazy ran his tongue over the edge of his yellow-stained teeth and reached for another slab of rock. As he laid the slab in place on the wall, he swept his eyes over the two-hundred-foot-square prison compound enclosed by a ten-foot-high stone wall. It was a bare fraction of the size of the pen at Yuma, a rat hole of a prison. With the tall walls stopping all wind, it baked like a fry pan under the sun.

Past the south end of the cell block, on the opposite side of the prison yard, he saw a second guard standing in the shade of the mess hall. In the tower on the south wall, a third guard faced back toward the two on the ground. Between the three, they could see practically every inch of the enclosed compound.

The sergeant and the remaining two guards would be looking for coolness in their stone cabin outside the wall. Where the Quechan trackers were would be anybody's guess. They had built a small brush-and-stone shelter when the contingent of prisoners and guards had first arrived at the site. They seldom used it now. But they would be close enough to hear a pistol shot or the heavy bell used to signal an escape.

Crazy dropped his head and began to work on the wall again. Every day since he had walked through the iron gates of Yuma Prison, he had thought of only one thing. Escape. He had obeyed every rule, controlled his quick temper, and did not strike back at the cruelty. In March when they had chained him like a dog to the tail end of a wagon and marched him into the desert, he had begun his plan to escape.

And today of all days he could not afford to be locked up. Only one more step of his plan remained to be accomplished. If he pulled it off, all would be ready for him to go over the wall tonight.

"That's the last of the rock, Guard Al," called Crazy to the guard by the commissary. "Is it all right if I go fetch another wagon load?"

"If it's okay with the guard at the gate," growled Al.

Caloon filled a half-gallon canteen at the spring and walked to the wagon to toss the water into the bed and close the tailgate. He moved into the deep shadow of the stables and leaned against one of the upright supports. The pungent smell of the sweaty horses and fresh manure lay heavy in the heat.

The odors recalled pleasant memories for Crazy. They reminded him of happy times before his son had been shot down in a burst of gunfire by two drunken cowboys firing blindly along a street in Tucson. And he, in terrible grief and anger, had rushed from his livery stable, walked straight into the men, and shot them dead with his six-gun before half a hundred witnesses.

Crazy forced away the sad memories and lifted his head.

He breathed deeply of the familiar aromas of the stable and felt as if he were already half free. Within a very short time he would be completely free. Or dead.

He threw harness upon the backs of the two horses, backed them into position in front of the wagon and hooked up the traces. He clucked the reluctant team of animals out into the bright sunlight and reined them in the direction of the south gate.

A slight puff of air drifted in through the open window of the guard tower and stirred the superheated air. The guard twisted about to face toward the breeze and pulled his sweaty shirt open to allow the air to cool him. He shaded his eyes and scanned the shimmering, heat-distorted plain stretching away mile after mile to the west and the distant Colorado River, and Yuma, and the women. The wind died away to nothing and the man cursed.

The crunch of approaching iron wagon wheels on the rock and grit of the prison yard drew the guard's attention. As he swung around, he picked up the .44-40 Winchester from where it leaned against the wall and held it ready.

"Guard Tom, I need another load of stone to finish the wall of the new guardhouse," Crazy called up from below. "Guard Al said I could go get it if you thought it was all right." Caloon grinned his silly grin, stretching his lips thin as paper across his teeth.

"You're a dumb son of a bitch, you know that, Crazy? Why in hell do you keep bothering people when it's so goddamn hot?" Tom leaned out the window, shifted a great quid of tobacco, and spat brown juice down toward the prisoner.

Crazy felt the spray of spittle on his face and his gray eyes hardened into icy marbles. The foolish grin remained on his lips and he laughed his short squirrel chatter, high and jerky, as he played the lamebrain.

"Just trying to earn my keep, Guard Tom," he said.

"Go get your load of stone. But you had better remember the 'dead wire.' One step beyond it and I'll blow your head off."

The guard lifted a long iron bar, sliding it vertically upward until it was free of a series of overlapping iron rings that extended up the full height of the gate. The two half portals began to swing slowly apart. Only from the guard tower could the gate be unlocked.

Crazy shoved the gates completely open and slapped the horses through. The animals, glad to be outside, broke into a trot along the dusty road, the empty wagon bouncing and rattling behind.

After giving the horses a quick look to measure their speed, Crazy pulled the gate shut and held it in alignment while the guard plunged the rod back down through the metal loops.

Crazy sprinted to catch the horses. His cowhide moccasins splattered and splashed the inch-deep dust, staining his pumping legs halfway to his knees with chocolate dirt.

He ran lightly, his shirt billowing in the breeze created by his own speed. His stride was long and effortless, his breathing slow and deep. The time was growing short. He could feel escape in the air—in every cell of his body.

As Crazy overhauled the wagon he scanned the wide expanse of land before him. The convicts had built their prison in a location selected by the sergeant on the north end of Castle Dome Plain where a small spring trickled out of the flint-like lava. That was the only source of water for twenty miles in any direction, the nearest being the Gila River, due south, and on the far side of a chain of mountain peaks barely visible in the distance.

Castle Dome Plain was the nearly flat, lower slopes of Castle Dome Mountain. The mountain's massive ramparts had been formed by molten rock pouring from great vents in the earth and spreading more than forty miles across the land. Then as the outer reaches of the flows hardened into solid rock, the lava had piled upward nearly three quarters of a mile, crowding the sky for space.

For many miles in all directions from the prison, the land was barren except for a scattering of tall saguaro cactus standing like giant sentinels and patches of stunted creosote and greasewood bushes. The terrain, scarred by numerous shallow washes, slanted downward at a low angle to the southeast until it was cut by the west-flowing Gila River.

Crazy caught up with the wagon and then moved ahead to run beside the team. The dust he and the horses roiled into the dead still air hung like a pall for several seconds before it settled back to the ground.

In the tower, the guard leaned the Winchester against the wall and picked up a .56 Spencer, his long-distance killer gun. He worked the action of the breech open until the brass shell slid into view, then rammed the lever back into place ready to fire. Maybe this time Crazy Caloon would make a mistake and cross the wire.

The "dead wire," a single strand of barbed wire hanging from rock mounds spaced two rods apart completely encircled the prison. The wire, new and glinting in the sunlight, sagged in deep drooping arcs between the piles of stone.

The guard knew the range to the wire, exactly three hundred yards. He had practiced with the gun at that distance. It was a moderately difficult shot, just far enough to make the placing of a bullet into a man's chest a sporting proposition.

Crazy reached out and caught the closer horse by its bridle, slowing it and its mate to a walk, and guided them off to the right. Two or three acres of flat black slabs of lava rock like the flaking skin of some giant reptile lay thickly on the surface of the ground.

The wagon gradually filled with rock as he worked farther and farther into the southwest corner of the fenced area. As he tossed another stone into the wagon, he surveyed the prison, its high walls framed against the hot yellow sky. He located the guard standing looking toward the wagon, the heavy Spencer hanging in the crook of his arm. He must be careful and not provoke the guard, for he had seen the man shoot.

Crazy was at the spot to which he had been working and he called a low command for the horses to stop. He must act now and hope the guard could not detect what was really being done.

He moved forward on the far side of the wagon opposite to the guard. Quickly he bent down and lifted three flat rocks, three or so feet on a side, and flopped them out of the way. A shallow trench nearly large enough to hold a man's body lay exposed.

With a broken leaf of a wagon spring he had used previously in excavating the hole, Crazy dug furiously, ripping and gouging at the ground. He scooped out the loosened dirt with his hands, tossing the dry soil away, hiding it among the rocks so there was no evidence of his labor.

A few minutes later he stopped digging. The hole was big enough now, six feet long and more than a foot deep. Crazy picked up a rock and made a show of loading it in the bed of the wagon. As he deposited it, he grabbed the canteen and, holding it pressed to his side, returned to the excavation. He placed it with a smaller canteen already there.

Swiftly he laid the three rocks back into position, bridging and concealing the result of his labor. He felt good; he had done it. He cackled his shrill laugh.

The guard heard Crazy's laughter floating across the distance. It sounded happy. How could anyone in his right mind be happy working as a prisoner under such a scorching sun? But then Crazy Caloon was not sane.

In the cell behind the iron-barred door there was a stirring and rustling like a den of snakes as the thirty prisoners tossed restlessly on their straw ticks lying on the dirt floor. Now and then one of the men babbled a few words, mostly unintelligible, in his sleep.

It was after midnight, yet the rock walls of the cell still radiated heat. Not a breath of air had found entry through the small, barred windows to sweep away the heat from the burning day not long ended.

Crazy Caloon lay motionless, silent, too charged with the excitement of his escape to sleep. Sweat pooled in the hollows below his eyes as he waited, staring upward at the ceiling, invisible in the pitch-black darkness.

Hours later, impatience prodding him, Crazy climbed silently to his feet and slipped to the window on the north side of the cell. He looked out between the bars at the Big Dipper, measuring its position in relation to the polestar. He judged the time to be three o'clock in the morning. Time to make his try for his long anticipated freedom.

He moved toward the end of the cell containing the door, passing the two empty beds that had once been used by the Mexicans, Ortego and Bastamente. They were dead now, buried outside the prison.

The two Mexicans had seized upon the last day before the tall perimeter was completed, locking them inside, to make their bid for escape. While they were gathering stone outside the prison, a dust storm had whipped in from the west. Under cover of the blowing dust, they had quickly unhooked the wagon from the horses, jumped astride the animals, and raced for Mexico, fifty miles south.

When the dust had blown itself away to the east and the guard gave the alarm, the Mexicans had had an hour's head start. The Quechans gave chase, running effortlessly, trailing their short-barreled Winchesters and reading the signs of their quarry with ease.

Three days later Crazy saw the Quechans reappear at the prison, riding double on one horse with the dead Mexicans tied across the second like sides of beef. The bounty hunters dismounted and without a word stalked away to their crude shelter and fell into their blankets. The next day they collected their gold coins from the sergeant.

Feeling the side of the cell carefully with his fingers as he slipped through the darkness, Crazy found the long slab of rock in the wall ten feet from the iron-barred door. He had laid that very stone more than five months before. The score or more of smaller rocks below it bore no weight of the wall and only dry dirt, instead of mud mortar, filled the joints between them.

Noiselessly he pulled and pried at the stone directly below the larger slab. The rock pulled free in his hands. Silently he laid it on the floor and removed several others, the long slab continuing to bridge the growing opening.

"Kill the damn guard," muttered a prisoner from the darkness.

Crazy snapped a look down the length of the cell. The other prisoners must not awaken, for surely some of them would demand to try to escape with him. That would destroy any chance for success.

"What's the matter? Don't you want to get out of this damn hellhole?" asked the same voice. Then the man began to mumble incomprehensibly, his voice guided by a tormented, dreaming brain.

Crazy breathed again, with relief. Quickly he took two more stones out of the wall. The hole was large enough. He squatted down and shoved his head through to the outside.

The prison yard lay quiet. Weakly lighted by a half-moon, the partially finished walls of the new guardhouse were faintly visible a stone's throw away.

A horse stamped the ground in the stable. Off to the left, a red spot glowed in the tower as the guard sucked on a cigarette.

Crazy eased his shoulders into the opening. They stuck in the tight fit. He applied a little pressure and slid through with a slight rattle of falling fragments of rock.

For several minutes he squatted on the ground, pressed tightly to the wall of the building, listening. With all the prisoners securely locked inside the cell, the guard in the tower should be the only man on duty. But Caloon's eyes searched every foot, every murky outline, for danger.

Then he moved, a dark shadow among other dark shadows, gliding in a crouch to the northwest corner of the tall barrier that caged him away from freedom.

In the roughly constructed stone wall, Crazy's searching fingertips found a hold and he began to hoist himself up the wall. At the top, he slid across on his stomach so as not to be silhouetted against the moonlit sky. Then he dropped to the ground outside.

He was free. He was outside and no guard with a large caliber rifle watched his every move. His heart thudded and an overpowering impulse to race away into the night assailed him. His muscles tensed in readiness for the first lunge.

With all his will, he fought the urge. His original plan must be followed. Though he felt strong, he was no match for the Quechans. Even with the three hours until daylight as a head start, they would easily overhaul him. They had been known to run two hundred miles and pull a prisoner down. And to be caught by them meant death.

Crazy moved away slowly, carefully stepping on the stones lying on the ground. They were barely discernible. Sometimes he squatted down to reach out and feel the dim

outlines to make certain they were indeed rock. For there
was an excellent chance the eagle-eyed Indians would find
the imprint if his moccasins touched the dirt.

As he searched for rocks to walk upon, he deliberately
made a large arc, circling far out and away from the prison
to keep a great distance between himself and the guard. He
stopped often to examine the tower, but there was no
movement there.

Crazy came at last to the trench he had dug in the ground.
The first stone, then the second, were lifted aside. As he
took hold of the last, the deadly warning rattle of a snake
exploded in his face.

He jerked back and almost cried out. Catching his startled
reflex, he held himself rigid. The damn snake must have
crawled into the excavation to get out of the hot sun and
now was warning him to find another place.

He scooped up a handful of dirt and pebbles and hurled it
into the blackness beneath the stone. The rattle instantly
stopped as the snake struck. The serpent coiled for the next
strike. Then the rattle began again, quickly increasing in
rapidity until it was one whirring buzz of sound.

At the second blow of thrown dirt, the snake slithered up
out of the hole. With its sensuous body, a wiggling shadow
barely visible among the rocks, the snake speedily retreated
into the gloom.

The last stone was slid aside. Crazy scrutinized the
trench, looking for any form that would identify a second
intruder. There was nothing but the dark outlines of the
canteens.

Crazy sat in the darkness and watched the moon and stars
arc through the heavens. A pack of coyotes yapped a high,
clear chorus on the high ridges of the mountain above the
prison. A large ghostly night flyer, spotting Crazy's dark
bulk on the ground, dropped down from the black velvet

sky to investigate. Crazy heard the swish of the air past the diving body, heard the rustle of feathers as the bird altered the set of its wings and tail to maintain its course. He caught one glimpse of the hurtling body as it bottomed its fall and swept upward, not to reappear.

The wild flight of the bird caused a bright flame of happiness to spring to life in Crazy's heart. For the first time he thought he might really make good his escape.

The Big Dipper wheeled around the North Star, marking off the remaining hours of the night. Before dawn showed first light, Crazy crept into the shallow hole. Reaching out, he brushed away the tracks on the ground and then carefully placed the stones to bridge the excavation.

He lay on his back and breathed deeply of the smell of the rock and the dry dirt. He hoped the pit would not end up being his grave. At the irony of the thought, he started his weird laugh but choked it off. There was no need for that. The game of playing the crazy was ended.

Chapter 4

The alarm bell within the tall stone walls of the prison began to ring frantically. The clang of the heavy iron bell swept through the cool morning air and jolted Caloon awake. He smiled to himself in the dim light of his hiding place and listened to the guards calling excitedly to each other. The first count of the prisoners for the day had been made and had come up one short. Crazy Caloon had escaped.

Slowly he raised the rock that hung close above his face and peered toward the source of the commotion. In the tower, the guard on duty scanned the brush and rock of the desert. His scrutiny missed the narrow crack under the uptilted rock and the alert foxy eyes staring out.

The two Quechan manhunters loped in at a fast pace and were quickly admitted through the iron-barred gate. Five minutes later they reemerged stripped down to buckskin loincloths, moccasins, knives in their belts, and trailing their short Winchester carbines.

Like a pair of hunting dogs, the Indians began a circle of the prison, inside the wire and about a hundred yards out from the walls. They moved swiftly and effortlessly, sniffing at the ground with their wise, experienced eyes.

Caloon lowered the stone into place above his face and pressed his ear against the ground. He remained perfectly silent and waited. Once he thought, just for a moment, he heard the muffled tread of feet striking the ground, but he was not sure.

The Indians found nothing in the first encirclement of the prison except sign from old work details. They expanded their search pattern, moving beyond the wire.

Caloon heard the thud of their running feet striking the ground and rapidly approaching his hiding place. This was the time of greatest peril. Had he left any tracks, any sign that would betray him? They must not discover him or he would die.

The footfalls passed close, too damn close, just outside the wire. Then they faded away.

Caloon let his breath out in a sigh and pried up the stone to look. He spotted the Indians, their rope-like muscles rippling beneath dark copper skin, race away, dodging through the saguaro and brush. They dropped down into a gully and disappeared.

The Quechans made a third turn of the prison and then began to course back and forth in wide sweeps on the south and west. Caloon could see them now and then and he knew their strategy. The nearest water, other than the spring inside the prison walls, was the Gila River lying to the south or the Colorado River at a slightly greater distance to the west. An escaping prisoner would almost certainly have to take one of those directions.

Caloon completely lost sight of the Indians as they worked farther away. He propped the stone up with a small rock, made himself as comfortable as possible, and lay watching for them to return.

About mid-morning the bounty hunters came running in

from the desert and entered the prison. They left almost immediately to the west, mounted on horseback and with small packs tied behind the saddles. Caloon nodded his understanding. They had found no sign and now would ride rapidly to the Colorado. Once there, they would stake out their tired horses in some hidden canyon and patrol the river on foot until they found him. Or decided he had gone to the Gila River and transferred their search to that water source.

Caloon lay back and tried to relax. The stone above him grew hot as the wall of an oven and heat poured down on him. He began to sweat. It would be a terrible day.

The brown spires of the desert mountain reared above Spring Creek in a high, jagged silhouette against the pale blue sky. At the bottom of the mountain, narrow brush-covered foothills radiated outward. Like the outstretched talons of a giant eagle, they pierced deeply into the valley of the San Cristóbal Desert. On the slopes between the rocky crest of the mountain and the rim of the desert, dried bunch clothed the steep land like a yellowish-brown blanket.

Lava ledges jutted out like bare ribs from half a dozen locations on the flanks of the mountains. On those bony prominences the eagles perched and the bobcats came out in the cool of the evening to lie and watch the sun go down while they waited for the darkness to fall and the night-long hunt to begin.

Russ Tarlow carried a double-barreled 12-gauge shotgun as he hunted quietly along the ridge of the hill that extended to the north in the direction of the Gila River. Early in the spring he had seen quail chicks, no larger than his thumb, watering with a nervous hen at the creek. By this late in the summer, the young quail should be nearly grown and would make a delicious fry.

Russ skimmed his eyes over the hillside searching for the birds' hiding place. He knew that somewhere he would find them coveyed up in the shade beneath a brush or ledge of rock.

On Russ's left two birds spurted upward from under a palo verde tree. They darted away, their beating wings a noisy whirr of power.

The shotgun came up to Russ's shoulder without conscious thought. He shot the quail flying straight away from him first, the bird dying in a bursting cloud of feathers. Then he pivoted and fired upon the second bird, killing it before the first had struck the ground.

He did not reload, for these two shots had been the last shells for the shotgun. But that was all right for his father would return soon and they would go to Yuma and buy a new supply of ammunition. He moved forward to recover the fallen quail.

A third bird exploded from cover, its wings flailing the hot air, pumping upward. Russ tossed the empty shotgun to his left hand and stabbed for his six-gun. He drew, pointed the gun by instinct, and fired.

The strong gray wings ceased their hurried thrusts as the bullet knocked the bird into a cartwheeling tumble. It plummeted to earth.

Russ grinned in appreciation of the shot. Much practice under the critical eye of his father had gone into making his hand so skillful. But Russ knew some luck was involved in hitting the small moving target at that long range.

He retrieved the birds and walked to the rim of the hill to look down into the valley. Even though he knew robbers and rustlers roamed the newly settled Arizona Territory, he paused in admiration of the beauty of the view. A warm, secure feeling took hold of him as he ran his eyes over what he and his family had created.

A quarter mile away and five hundred feet below him, a house, constructed of stone to last, nestled beside the flowing water of Spring Creek. He was proud of the house, mostly built by himself with only an occasional stint of help from his father.

Upstream from the house a few hundred yards, Russ had piled boulders across the creek bed, partially damming the stream. From the pool backed up behind the rocks, water was shunted into an irrigation ditch.

The ditch had been dug by hand with great labor over many weeks. Now it carried the water at a gentle gradient, holding the precious liquid high on the slope, positioning it to water the fertile soils of the benchland.

Near the house a portion of the water was released to irrigate a garden and a small orchard. Farther downstream an emerald-green patch of meadow, nearly thirty acres, was nourished by the remainder of the water, which flooded over it in scores of hand-dug corrugations.

The creek was the center of life for the ranch. Its waters were birthed on the high reaches of the mountain where a layer of rhyolite lava outcropped. The impervious rhyolite forced the cool liquid that percolated down through the hidden crevices and faults inside the mountain to emerge from its dark passageways and gush forth as a mighty spring.

Over the millennium, the cascading water had carved a deep plunging channel down the rocky flank of the mountain. Cottonwood and willow lined the valley from the stream's headwaters to the desert floor.

Downstream from the ranch, the stream disappeared into the deep sand and gravel of the valley bottoms, sinking down through the porous rubble and flowing along the top of the bedrock until it reemerged forty miles away as another spring in the bottom of the Gila.

The ranch was prospering. During the four years Russ and his parents had lived in the valley, their herd of cattle had increased from sixty head to over two hundred. He and his father had ambitiously talked of enlarging the herd to a thousand head.

Jack Tarlow was a horse trader, often gone for days at a time. He knew horses and was a good trader, almost always returning home with substantial sums of money. Often he brought expensive gifts to Russ and his mother.

Russ pulled one of those presents, a brass-tubed telescope, from his pocket. Extending it full length, he glassed down at the ranch house.

His mother came out of the front door and began to hang wash on the clothesline fastened between two cottonwoods. Miniaturized by the distance, she was a tiny doll dressed in blue gingham. Russ almost called out to her, telling of his success with the quail, but decided it was too far for a voice to carry.

He swung his magnifying glass to the mountain. The cattle were on the summer range. He located several scattered about in the bunch grass on the high upper slope.

Three buzzards floated into the field of view of the telescope. Circling around and around with their wings fixed and stiff, the birds were augering in on the scent of something dead. Carefully Russ marked the location. When it grew cooler in the evening, he would ride up and take a look.

He glanced in the opposite direction toward the San Cristóbal Desert. His father was a week overdue from his planned date of return and Russ was concerned. But his father was a master with either a six-gun or rifle and should be safe.

Perhaps he could see his father returning if he went to the north end of the hill about two miles away. From that vantage point he would be able to see for a long distance. He placed the quail in the shade of a bush, leaned the shotgun in the fork of a limb, and headed down the ridge.

Russ found a seat in the narrow shade of an ancient

saguaro cactus and methodically scanned the harsh brilliance of the San Cristóbal with his telescope. Heat like swirling liquid streamed up from the desolate desert that stretched before him for two score miles or more. The tall saguaro that studded the desert floor and the distant mountains on the far side were twisted and contorted by the shimmering heat waves that poured up from the hot earth.

Something moved into the zone of magnification of the telescope—a black spot far out, miles away. It was an apparition of the heat waves that vanished only to reappear, that bobbed up and down and wound in and out between the trunks of the giant saguaro.

Russ watched the object intently. It slowly grew, heading directly toward him. It appeared to be following the main trail that came in from Tucson. If it continued on that route, it would pass just below him near the creek at the base of the hill.

Russ's eyes strained and watered from the intensity of his scrutiny. Finally he was certain. The moving object was a gray horse without a rider.

His father rode a gray horse and Russ was greatly worried. He lowered the telescope to rest his eyes for a few seconds. Then once again he focused the glass on the horse.

Russ's heart jumped, for he could see the outline of a man leaning forward from the saddle and lying along the neck of the horse.

Two new riders appeared in the edge of the field of the telescope. Russ centered the eye of the glass on them. They were about a mile behind the gray horse and pushing their animals. He measured the progress of the two horsemen and knew they were gaining on the first rider.

Russ moved the scope to bear on the first horse. It was much closer now. The rider still clung to the neck of his mount.

And then in the bright sunlight and under the magnification of the telescope, dark red blood became visible, staining the shirt of the man. And the side of the horse carried a large splotch of blood.

Russ stood up, ready to rush down the side of the hill to help his father. But he quickly lowered himself back to the ground. The outlaws who had shot his father and now pursued him to his very home had to be stopped. They must not find the ranch, must not find his mother.

The gray horse walked steadily along, carrying its wounded rider. They passed below Russ, not a hundred yards away. The animal had found its way home without guidance, for the hands of the man clutched only the mane, the reins hanging loosely.

Russ turned angry eyes back to stab at the outlaws. They were less than a mile away and coming at a fast gallop, intent on overhauling his father. As Russ watched, men and horses followed the trail down into the creek crossing. The moment they disappeared from view, he sprang from his hiding place and dashed down the side of the hill.

Quickly he stepped behind a saguaro near the trail. His hand brushed some of the thousands of thorns on the cactus and he jerked back. He quieted his excited breathing and ignored the pain in his hand and waited. One thought burned his mind: the gunmen had to be made to turn away.

Russ threw a quick glance up the path in the direction his father had gone. Horse and rider were out of sight.

The iron-shod hooves of horses rattled the rocks in the bottom of the creek. Then the outlaws' mounts, puffing noisily from being pushed hard, climbed the bank.

The two horsemen rode into sight, towering above the brush not forty feet away. Russ stepped out from behind the cactus and pointed his six-gun at his father's enemies.

Both men saw Russ instantly. For a split second they measured the armed man blocking the trail, saw his youth and the scared, uncertain look on his face. The one on the left locked fierce eyes on Russ and drew his pistol unbelievably swiftly.

Without ever having seen such a savage look before, Russ knew the eyes spoke death. He fired. The gun bucked in his hand. The bullet smashed into the man's chest, rocking him in the saddle. Then he tumbled sideways to the ground.

Russ hurriedly swept his gun right to cover the second outlaw. That man's pistol was lining up on Russ, the wicked eye of the barrel nearly on target.

Firing more swiftly than he ever thought possible, Russ shot two bullets into the center of the man's chest.

Tiny puffs of dust erupted from the man's shirt as the hurtling chunks of lead slammed into him, driving him backward.

His vest flopped open and Russ saw a momentary glint of sunlight from metal on the man's chest.

The rider's feet came loose from the stirrups and he fell to the ground with a thump.

The horses of the men bolted out through the brush a short distance. They halted to stand snorting in fright at the fusillade of gunshots.

Russ dashed forward. He had to see what was on the man's shirt, to make sure. There could not be a badge. His eyes must be playing tricks on him.

He grabbed the fallen man and rolled him onto his back. The dying man's chest heaved and made a sucking sound. A bloody froth bubbled up to his lips.

A pair of hate-filled eyes stared at Russ for a handful of seconds. "Goddamn you to hell," whispered the man. Then he quivered and his head fell loosely to the side.

Russ snatched his hand away and rocked back on his heels, stunned. Controlling his reaction, he reached out and lifted the flap of the vest. A deputy U.S. marshal's badge was pinned to the blood-drenched shirt.

Russ hastened to the first man he had shot and knelt down beside the body. He found the tin star of a second deputy U.S. marshal in a shirt pocket.

Slowly he sank down on the ground and sat in the dust and shivered at the horrible mistake. He had gunned down two lawmen. But they must be the ones who had wounded his father. There was no doubt they were trailing him. But why? Why?

Russ jumped to his feet and hurried toward the horses. One of the animals snorted and trotted off as he drew close. He slowed his pace so as not to spook further the already frightened animals. One stood its ground, tossing its head nervously and watching him with the whites showing in its eyes. Russ caught the bridle and jumped into the saddle.

His breath rasped in his throat as he spurred toward the ranch house. There must be some terrible misunderstanding. His father could not be an outlaw.

Chapter 5

Russ pulled the horse down to a slow pace as he neared the ranch house and walked it in quietly. In the center of the yard he dismounted. His father's gray horse stood near the door, the dark splash of blood on its shoulder drying in the sun.

Moving noiselessly along the front of the house, Russ drew near the partially open door and halted. Inside he heard his mother's voice.

"Lay still, Jack. I must close the wound. The bullet went cleanly through your shoulder without hitting a bone, but you're bleeding badly."

A cloth ripped as his mother prepared a bandage. Then silence. Russ could see in his mind's eye his mother's gentle, sure hands tending the injured man.

Finally his father spoke in a weak voice. "Where's Russ?"

"Out quail hunting. I heard the shotgun far up on the ridge of the hill some time ago. He will be very upset when he finds out you've been shot."

"Russ must not know why I got shot. We'll tell him some

holdup men waylaid me for my money. That I escaped but they wounded me."

His mother said something in a voice so low Russ could not make it out.

Jack Tarlow spoke again. "I thought I had shaken the lawmen off my trail, but they found me just before daylight."

"Did they follow you here?"

"I don't know. I don't think so. But they found me in the dark. They are good, very good. The town of Tucson hired them about a month ago and they have jurisdiction to go anyplace in the Territory."

"Oh, Jack, why did you do it? We didn't need the money so badly that you had to rob somebody."

"You don't understand. There was this cattle buyer for a packing company who had a lot of money . . ."

Russ clutched at the stone wall. He was unable to believe what he had heard. His head buzzing, he whirled about and hastily retreated from the door.

A great anger burned within him. Two marshals lay dead in the dirt. Two lawmen killed by him because his father had lied when he said he traded horses for his money.

He stopped and stared down at the creek without seeing it. What tore at his heart most was the fact his mother had kept the terrible secret—his father was a common outlaw, a man who rode out and robbed with a gun.

The ranch had been built with stolen money. No, not all of the ranch. Four years of Russ's life and labor were buried in the stones of the house, in the long irrigation ditch and meadow, and the young calves.

Russ shook his head to clear it. Other U.S. marshals would come searching for their comrades. And whether or not Russ had shot them believing they were robbers who had shot his father would mean nothing to them.

He would be arrested and hung. And Jack Tarlow would

go to prison, or maybe he would also hang. For perhaps he had committed murder during some of his crimes.

Russ moved with determination. Outlaw or not, his father must remain free to care for his mother. The bodies of the lawmen had to be taken far away from the ranch and hidden. And then as a double protection he would ride on, laying an obvious trail. In that way he might pull those who came to search for the marshals after him, instead of after his father.

He circled to the rear of the house and stepped silently through the open window into his room. Quickly he found a piece of paper and stub of a pencil and leaned over the table to write.

There were many things he wanted to say to his parents: You lied to me and because of that I have killed. I am hurt and angry, but I still love you. To protect you I will carry away the dead lawmen and try to hide your crimes.

He wrote one word, "Good-bye," and signed it "Russ."

Hurriedly he gathered a few necessities and rolled them inside his bedroll. A box of shells for his .30-30 Winchester and two boxes for his six-gun placed in his saddlebags finished his packing. He picked up his rifle from where it stood in the corner.

Russ turned and surveyed his room for what he knew would be the last time. Many pleasant memories flooded through his mind. Beyond the door he heard his mother's kind voice, as he had heard it countless times before. For a moment he listened to the loved tones, then he left soundlessly by the window.

Briefly halting at the well, Russ filled a large canteen. Then astride his long-legged roan horse, and leading the dead lawman's animal, he headed down the creek.

Mounted on horseback, he easily caught the pony of the second lawman and headed in the direction of the ambush.

As he neared the site, all the horses pulled back at the smell of death and had to be forced up near the bodies.

He swung down and hoisted the loose-jointed corpses across their saddles and tied their arms and legs together beneath the bellies of the horses. To be sure the bodies would stay in place, he roped their belts to the pommels of the saddles. He kept the marshals' bedrolls, leaving them fastened behind the saddles.

Russ tied the head of one horse to the tail of the second and put a rope on the lead animal. He stepped astride his mount and, pulling the two reluctant horses with their load of death behind him, rode down into the creek bed.

In the middle of the stream, he stopped and allowed the animals to drink their fill. When they had finished, he kicked them ahead at a trot to the northeast, across the desert and toward the Gila River.

He threw a look upward to check the height of the sun. It rode its zenith, bright and hot. A long scorching day still remained to be ridden.

Russ never looked back.

The thunderheads had begun to build in mid-afternoon and drifted across the desert. By dusk, lightning lashed down from the towering cloud masses and Caloon heard the thunder rumbling over the stony crest of Dome Mountain.

The night hunters, the coyote, the bobcat, and the great horned owl did not go out to hunt when it grew dark. They remained in their rocky lairs, nervously watching the giant cloud monsters striding over the land and striking out with their terrible fiery lances.

Caloon lay in his hole in the ground and listened to the thunder overhead. Each time a lightning bolt struck down to smite the earth, he felt the jolt of the blow surge through the rock and dirt that entombed him.

Carefully he slid aside the rocks that had lain directly

above him throughout the day. The air, cooled and agitated by the approaching storm, dropped down into the hole and fanned his hot body. He felt dampness in the breeze, promising rain.

The dusk turned to night and Caloon rose up from the trench and looked about. A gigantic thunderhead was close, moving straight upon him and the prison. Deep within the churning cloud, yellow-and-orange lightning flashed back and forth like a witch's boiling cauldron.

Wind whipped out in mighty gusts from the base of the cloud. A few scattered drops of rain, tremendously large, began to pepper the ground and Caloon smelled the water on the dust.

Wicked lightning flashed, blinding him, and the thunder deafened him. His spirits soared with the energy of the storm and he turned his head up and laughed loudly, matching the rising violence.

He faced the prison and, raising both his fists, shook them savagely and cursed the goddamned guards. And then he began to laugh again, not crazily, but happily, his breast full of freedom.

The guard in the gun tower felt the structure tremble under the onslaught of the storm. He took one last hurried look out over the desert and reached to lift the trapdoor to climb down to safety.

Lightning seared the land as the giant cloud discharged its electrical load like an erupting sun. The titanic bolt of raw power hammered the mountain, shaking its very roots. The walls of the prison rocked. The world turned bright as day.

Frightened and shaken, the guard whirled about and looked out from the tower. He could see every brush and rock on the desert etched in sharp relief. And damned to be a whoremonger if he didn't see Crazy Caloon standing near the "dead wire," his long hair blowing in the wind. The long golden mane, charged with electricity, glowed like a large halo. The insane prisoner was wildly shaking his raised fist and laughing.

The light winked out and complete darkness obliterated all sight. The guard hunkered in frozen attention. No! It could not have been Crazy. He was miles away, running before the killer Quechan Indians.

The charge differential between the cloud and the ground built in a few seconds to an unendurable level. Lightning again exploded the air, making the night day. The guard swept the land with his harried eyes. It lay empty. Caloon was not there. Quickly the guard scurried down the ladder and dashed for the guardhouse.

No one would believe him when he told what he had seen. Wait, better yet, say nothing for they would laugh at him and call him a coward afraid of the storm. He nodded in agreement with himself and lunged through the door of the shack as a deluge of cold rain poured down from the heavens.

Caloon ran steadily south. The thunder rumbled on all sides of him and the lightning snapped and cracked, slicing in unpredictable paths between the black clouds and from the clouds to the earth.

Wind buffeted him. Cold rain fell heavily, washing away his tracks as rapidly as he made them. But his clothes and moccasins were soaked, weighing him down. His pumping lungs burned with the effort to maintain his pace.

The night wore on as he ran. The tumult of the storm worked its way noisily to the northeast. Two hours later he was clear of the wind and rain. His clothes began to dry and grew lighter. He lengthened his stride and raced through the night.

Two hours before dawn, Caloon crossed the last stretch of Castle Dome Plain and dropped down into the valley of the Gila River. His first goal had been reached and he felt good.

He slumped onto the sandy bank and rested, catching his wind. His sweat dried as he listened to the sounds of the night. The water of the river, slipping by like oil in the darkness, whispered softly and now and then threw silver winks of light at him as the moonbeams were caught just right by the wet undulating surface.

Some time later, he roused himself and climbed to his feet. Taking off all his clothes except for his moccasins, he stepped into the water, pleasantly cool now that the sun was gone, and began to wade across. His feet searched the sand-and-mud bottom for deep holes, but the stream in low flow in late summer rose no deeper than his waist.

He waded through the moderate current of the stream for more than a hundred yards. As he approached the far shore, he spied a dark rocky point of land extending out into the river just upstream from him. Even as he recognized the shadowy obstruction, and wondered what strange effects it might have on the flow and depth of the river, he stepped into a hole of water far over his head.

He thrust his clothes above his head as he went under and struck out strongly with his feet and free hand. He came up spitting silty water and facing back out toward the center of the stream.

As he treaded water, the dark scenery of the night revolved about him. A deep vortex of spinning water and suspended silt had been birthed in the lee of the point of land and he was being rotated around in it like a piece of driftwood.

During river flood stage the whirlpool would be deadly, but now it was of little danger to Caloon. Holding his clothing safe and dry above the water, he stroked and kicked free of the clutching fingers of the river and made his way to the shallows.

When the water was no deeper than his knees, he turned and made his way a mile upstream. He left the stream at a rocky ledge, crossed a game trail that ran along the edge of the river, and climbed up on a tall jutting rock. He put his clothes on, lay down, and relaxed his tired body. Sleep came immediately.

Caloon awoke. He remained perfectly motionless. The sound, a soft scuff of horses' hooves, had been more felt than heard. Then through the last darkness of the night, he heard an iron horseshoe clunk dully against a rock.

He rose to an elbow and looked downstream along the shore of the Gila. At first he was not certain he really saw the strange apparition, a cavalcade of horses drifting toward him through the murk.

A man rode the first horse and led two others. In the faint first glimmer of the dawn, the packs on the two trailing horses looked like dead men tied across the saddles.

Caloon sighed silently; coming straight toward him were the things he needed most—a horse, gun, and clothing. His for the taking. Silently, like a hungry lion, he crawled out onto the point of rock that overhung the trail and waited for the horse carrying the intended victim to come within reach.

The man rode with his head slumped forward in sleep and nodding to the step of his plodding mount. The horse tensed as his sharp animal ears heard the slight scrape of Caloon's moccasins bunching for the attack.

The mustang's night eyes darted upward to the top of the rock and saw the crouching menace ready to leap. The horse snorted in fright. The rider jerked awake.

Caloon sprang off the rock, plunging downward. His prey, alerted by the sudden alarm of the horse, reacted swiftly. He threw up a stiff arm to fend off the attacker and at the same time tried to duck out of the way.

Caloon's hurtling body rammed through the defense. His shoulder struck hard and his arm encircled the quarry, ripping him from the saddle.

They fell heavily into the shallow water of the river with Caloon on top. Caloon sprang immediately to his feet and, as the strange rider staggered up, savagely slugged him on the side of the head, knocking him into deeper water.

Caloon hurled himself upon the man, mostly submerged in the water, and clamped his powerful hands on the man's throat. He shoved the face beneath the water and held it there.

The man lashed out, striking up out of the water with his fist, and his feet thrashed. But his counterattack was confused and ineffective and Caloon continued to hold him under. Finally the frantic actions stopped as if the man had given up or lost consciousness.

Suddenly two hands shot up out of the water and encircled Caloon's neck. He strained to break free, but the vising hands held firmly and the thumbs stabbed inward, striving to crush and collapse his windpipe. Then the man pulled mightily and Caloon was yanked under the water with him.

Locked together, the two men rolled and tumbled down the stream with the current. Their kicking feet churned the water and roiled up the mud from the river bottom. In the rising sun their death battle created a dirty yellow blemish on the pristine water.

Caloon's breath had been drawn later than his opponent's and he knew he could last longer. So he clenched his grip tighter on the man's throat and fought to hold him under.

The hands clamped on Caloon's neck weakened and fell away. Caloon stood up, shoved his head into the life-giving air, and took a great draught. But he continued to hold his victim's face a few inches below the surface of the water.

The bright rays of the sun shined down, piercing the silty water and illuminating the long blond hair of the man he held there. The dead eyes stared upward accusingly from the water. For one terrifying second, Caloon thought he recognized the hair, so much like his own, and the face submerged in the mud looked ghostly familiar.

Frantically he lifted the man up from the river and shook the body like a large limp doll. Then splashing in great strides, Caloon rushed with the body to the bank.

He laid the man on his stomach, stepped astraddle of him, and, grabbing his wide belt, hoisted him nearly a yard off the ground. Water gushed from the lungs and mouth. Caloon dropped the body only to jerk it up forcefully again and hold it there while the water drained out the open mouth.

The body lay flat, face turned out of the dirt, and Caloon vigorously and rhythmically pumped the lungs by pressing and then releasing the broad back. One minute dragged into two.

A mighty spasm convulsed the body, immediately followed by a great belch of water. The lungs began to expand and contract on their own, sucking starvingly at the air.

Caloon moved hurriedly away from the body, as if now that it was once again alive, he did not want to touch it. He found a spot on the ground and sat watching the man revive.

Caloon could see the face clearly and for a long time he sat and sadly looked at it. For that one fraction of a second in the water, he had thought the man was his son. But his son was dead, had been for more than two years. Only the striking resemblance between the two young men had saved this one's life, for Caloon knew he had meant to kill.

Chapter 6

·····················

Russ came to consciousness slowly, floating upward through a completely black and endlessly deep pool of water. His throat and lungs were on fire, yet he was freezing.

He shivered and a few seconds thereafter, he felt a blanket being draped across him and strong hands rolling him into its wool warmth. Russ let himself slide off into a troubled and jumpy sleep.

In a period of time that seemed only a short nap, Russ heard a man's voice speak near him. "Hey, fellow, are you going to sleep the whole morning away?"

Russ stirred, struggling to drag himself into wakefulness.

The voice continued. "I have many things to do and I should be many miles from here by now."

Haltingly Russ unwrapped himself from the blanket and sat up. Every muscle in his body felt bruised and strained and his hands trembled with weakness. He forced his eyes into focus and looked about. He was on the sandy bank of the river near the water.

A warm wind blew and the dark green leaves of a

cottonwood rustled close overhead. The smell of the water and mud of the river drifted to him, surprisingly strong.

Russ's eyes came to rest on a large man squatting nearby, looking at him. He measured the bony bulk and the weather-beaten face of the man, remembering the great strength and quickness of the large muscular hands that had almost killed him. In the man's eyes there was a sorrowful expression that Russ did not understand.

Russ propped himself up with his hands on the ground. "I take it you're the one that jumped me and tried to drown me in the river."

"Yep," answered Caloon, "and I'm real sorry about that."

They sat staring at each other across the few feet that separated them. The seconds dragged past and neither spoke.

Finally Caloon chucked a thumb over his shoulder at the horses and the grisly burdens they still carried. "I looked at those bodies you got tied to the horses. What are you doing with two dead deputy marshals?"

Russ did not respond for a moment, holding the man's look. Then he answered with a question. "Why did you jump a stranger and try to kill him?"

Caloon grinned ruefully. "Fair enough that I answer your question first. My name is Caloon and a couple of days ago I escaped from a prison the superintendent at Yuma had built up that way some twenty miles." He gestured with his hand to the north. "I need a gun and horse," continued Caloon. "Will you loan me those things?"

"You could have taken them and been long gone by now. Why did you stick around?"

"I hurt you bad and wanted to be sure you were all right. Now what's the story about the dead lawmen? If you plan to tell me, that is."

Russ examined the escaped convict, noting the dirty

prison garb of brown-and-white striped cotton trousers and shirt, and the man's body slumped, calm and relaxed. But there was a nervous twitch in the faded blue eyes.

"I made a mistake," said Russ. "Thought they were outlaws trying to rob and kill my dad. After I shot them, I found out different."

"That's a mighty short answer," said Caloon. "And that must have been some fancy shooting, for both of them were shot in the front. And now, I suppose you're looking for a safe place to hide them, eh?"

"Something like that," answered Russ. "You can take whatever you want. They don't have any use for any of their gear. I don't need any and wouldn't want it even if I did. You'll find a couple of hats jammed in one of the saddlebags."

Caloon moved to the loaded horses and circled around them, measuring the height and weight of the dead men. "This one looks about my size."

He loosened the ropes that held the body to the saddle, letting it tumble to the ground. Quickly he pulled the boots off. Next he removed the vest, pants, and shirt and tossed all into the water. He waded in, caught the garments as they started to float away and began to scrub the blood and sweat from them with sand from the river bottom.

Russ watched the man, hunkered in the river, the seat of his pants occasionally dipping down into the wetness and then dribbling water when he rose slightly.

"I could use some soap," said Caloon, glancing over his shoulder.

Russ did not respond. He felt overwhelmed. His world had been destroyed, switched from a gentle routine of cutting hay and moving cattle from one grassy ridge to another, to a hell of violence where he had killed two men and ridden all night with their bodies stinking of death. Now this strange man who had beaten him terribly and tried to drown him coolly washed one of the dead men's clothing in preparation for wearing them.

Five minutes later, Caloon had the clothing hanging on the limb of a cottonwood and drying in the breeze.

He turned to Russ. "I don't think you want to pack those bodies any further. Is that right?"

Russ nodded in the affirmative.

"Then let's bury them over there a couple hundred yards at the base of that rocky hill. That's far enough off the trail. They'll never be found and there's plenty of loose stones to cover them deep."

They dug a shallow grave with sharp-pointed lengths of driftwood. After placing the two lawmen in the hole, they scraped back the dirt, stomping it down firmly. Then they piled heavy rocks over the grave, placing the slabs so they appeared reasonably like a rock slide that had fallen from above.

"A good job," observed Caloon, backing up and surveying their work. He turned and looked at Russ. "I might not be a gent you would want to ride with, being I tried to kill you. And even more the law and at least two bounty hunters are after me, but you are welcome to travel with me for a distance if you want."

"Which direction you going?"

"If it really matters, I'm heading to the north, maybe a little northeast."

"It doesn't matter. One way is as good as any other," said Russ and looked in the direction the man had mentioned. He faced back toward Caloon. "And I'll go with you a ways. My name is Russ."

"All right, Russ. My name is Caloon. Let me get dressed and we'll be on our way."

Caloon walked toward the clothes hanging on the limb of the cottonwood. As he came near the water, he pulled one of the deputy marshal's badges from his pocket and with a flat, looping swing of his long arm, sent the metal disk skipping a long distance along the surface of the river. The spinning plate lost its momentum, its skimming hops becoming closer and closer together until it stopped and with hardly a ripple sank from sight.

Caloon pivoted to look at Russ and chuckled. "That's exactly how much of a splash those two dead lawmen will make, or for that matter, we will make when we go."

Caloon put on the damp clothes and struggled into a pair of boots. He fished the hats from the saddlebag Russ had indicated, selected the nearest fit, and shaped it best he could. Silently he strapped on a belt and holstered a six-gun.

He slowly drew the gun from the holster, cocked it, and pointed at a rock lying on the bank. He repeated the action, holstering, drawing, and aiming the weapon at a target. And Caloon repeated the draw again and again, each time increasing his speed.

Russ moved to his horse and began to replace the cartridges that had been in his six-gun and belt when he had gone into the river with fresh ammunition from his pack. As he did so he watched Caloon practice. Watched the movement of his hand become swift, the draw becoming smooth, effortless, and pointing very accurately at the selected targets.

"We have plenty of cartridges if you want to fire a few practice rounds," said Russ.

"No, not now," said Caloon, holstering his pistol. "It's dangerous here. There could be enemies nearby. Let's pack all the extra gear on the spare horse and ride out."

"These horses have traveled all night and are tired. We'll need a place to lay up and rest before too many miles more."

Caloon nodded and expertly tied the packs to one of the lawmen's mounts. He swung into the saddle of the second animal and, leading the packhorse, rode down into the river. Russ climbed aboard his roan and crossed the Gila beside Caloon.

They topped out on the bench above the river and halted for a moment to look to the north at the tall Palomas Mountains lying ten miles or so away. Then they struck out across the broad flood plain of the river, holding a course that would take them just east of the base of the dark volcanic mountains.

Heat was building rapidly and they rode at a moderate pace, winding around the brush and saguaro cactus. Caloon restlessly searched the land. He spoke to Russ. "If you see anything strange, anything at all, let me know."

"I'll do that," answered Russ.

Off to the right of the two men, a steep rocky hill jutted upward against the light blue sky. At the base of the hill, Gray Antelope ran swiftly, holding below a low ridge that cut across the valley. Big Wolf ran silently behind him.

From their lookout on the peak of the hill, the Quechans had seen the two men ride up out of the river bottom. In another minute the Indians would intersect the route of the two horsemen. Perhaps the white men had seen the escaped convict called Crazy Caloon and could give directions to find him.

Gray Antelope knew he and Big Wolf would have to approach the white men cautiously, yet openly. Renegade Indians still hid in the mountains and made raids down into the valleys to kill travelers and loot isolated ranches. The men might begin shooting upon first sight of two armed Indians, misinterpreting the reason for their approach, judging it to be one of attack. Even if the men would talk with them, they might not give information about another white man to an Indian.

The two Indians slowed and finally stopped to stand

quietly. Gray Antelope could see the two men but they had not yet discovered him. He stepped from the brush and into the trail of the horsemen. He held his rifle in his left hand and raised his right in a sign of friendly greeting. Big Wolf also moved into full view of the white men and about a hundred feet behind Gray Antelope. He stood alert and watching, holding his rifle ready.

Russ and Caloon pulled their horses to a quick halt. Caloon reined his mount slightly to the left and moved his hand near his six-gun.

He was surprised to see the Quechans here. The last time he had seen them they were on a fast pace toward the Colorado River. But now he knew the Indians' strategy, their hurried departure from the prison to the west had been a ruse, a trick to throw anyone watching off the true direction they planned to take.

Gray Antelope swept his eyes over the two horsemen and then fixed his questioning gaze on the older one. The man seemed faintly familiar.

"We look Yuma prisoner escape two days ago," said Gray Antelope. "You see?"

Caloon smiled from under the broad brim of his new hat, showing his teeth in a coyote grin.

Sudden recognition of the white man's strange smile burst into Gray Antelope's mind. "Crazy Caloon!" he cried in warning to Big Wolf and jerked his rifle up to his shoulder.

Caloon drew and fired in one blurred movement. The bullet slammed into Gray Antelope's chest, driving him down onto the rock and dust. Caloon swung the barrel of his pistol to point at the second Indian.

The range was long for a snap shot, maybe too long. But he had no time to hesitate; the Indian's rifle was now at his shoulder, the wicked eye of the barrel seeking a target.

Caloon fired, saw the Indian flinch as the bullet skittered along his ribs. Fired again and the Indian staggered backward, still trying to line up the sights of his rifle on Caloon. The white man emptied his gun into the brown skin of the reeling Indian.

Big Wolf, blinded by the shock of the bullets tearing into his body, collided with the thorn-laden trunk of a saguaro cactus. He did not feel the hundreds of piercing spines. Slowly he collapsed against the base of the giant cactus and died.

Russ sat stunned at the rapidity and violence of the killings. His hand had not touched his weapon. But what had the Indian screamed to his companion? What had he called Caloon? Had he said "Crazy"? Was he riding with an insane man?

Caloon turned and looked at Russ, noting the expression of shock and suspicion on the young man's face. It bothered Caloon, that mistrust, and while he reloaded he spoke, trying to explain.

"Those murdering, bounty hunting Quechans won't kill another prisoner in this world."

He climbed down from his horse and went to search the Indians. From small pouches fastened to their belts, he extracted four gold coins. After taking their knives and rifles, he went to the spare horse, untied the pack behind the saddle, and retied it, enclosing the weapons.

"Extra weapons always come in handy," Caloon said to Russ. He hoisted himself astride his horse and kicked him ahead. "I feel damned lucky those Quechans didn't come across me before I got hold of a gun."

As they rode past the two bodies sprawled in the dirt, Caloon spoke again. "It appears I haven't lost my shooting eye." But to himself he admitted his shot at the first Indian was a hand's width farther right than he had intended.

Russ touched the butt of his holstered six-gun. Never again, he vowed, would he be caught by surprise by what this strange, maybe insane man did.

Near noon Russ and Caloon found a brush-and-grass-covered marsh area of three or four acres where the rim of the valley met the base of the Palomas Mountains. They halted their tired horses and for several minutes sat cautiously, probing with wary eyes the two-hundred-yard-long expanse of green vegetation.

On the left and slightly above them, the spring that watered the meadow bubbled out on top of a lava outcrop. The water splashed down over the face of the rock, wetting it to reflect glassy in the sunlight.

Two dozen cottonwoods, very old and with thick trunks, grew clumped together in some deeper soil on the far side of the wetland. On the topmost branch of the tallest tree a large gray hawk with a white band on its tail watched with suspicious eyes every move of the humans. His beaked head swiveled from side to side and the compact body squatted against his roost, the wings tensed for flight.

At last, bothered beyond endurance by the closeness of the intruders, the hawk launched himself into the wind. His wings pumping powerfully, he climbed the hot air. Then, fully airborne, he turned directly away from the men and was soon lost from sight.

Finally, reasonably certain there was no danger, the two outlaws rode in under the cottonwoods and dumped their packs and saddles. After staking out the horses on the end of their lariats, they lay down in the shade of one of the giant cottonwood trees.

Russ wiped the sweat from his forehead and placed his pistol near his hand. He rested on his back, looking up into the branches of the tree.

A fine mist of water droplets, invisible to the eye and only felt, rained down from the thousands of leaves of the ancient tree. Striving vainly to keep its temperature low enough to survive under the burning sun, the moisture-loving tree sucked hundreds of gallons of water into its roots from the soaked soil, lifted it up the live inner layer of its bark, and allowed it to evaporate out through millions of pores on the underside of its leaves. The miniature rain fell cool and comforting on Russ.

Russ spoke to Caloon without looking. "I would say you know where you are heading. You haven't deviated a degree from a course that will take us to that big range of mountains on the skyline to the north."

"You're right," responded Caloon.

"What's up there?"

"Those mountains are the Kofas. And Raasleer, the most daring and successful cattle rustler in the Arizona Territory, rules them. I expect to join him."

"Rustling cattle doesn't seem like a very good way to spend the rest of your life," said Russ.

"I plan to do it just for a year or so. Long enough to get a small stake and then I'm off to Montana."

"What size gang does he have?"

"A large one, but it varies in number and, like most outlaw gangs, many of the members change over time. Some are always leaving with part of them coming back from time to time. And a few new ones keep coming to join. I hear he has a bunch of about five or six men that more or less make up the permanent core of his gang."

"It appears to me they'd be suspicious of newcomers. Will they just let us ride up and join?"

"No. Someone Raasleer trusts will have to vouch for me and then I'll vouch for you. About a year ago a fellow I know, named Tanwell, was released from Yuma Pen. I think he's with Raasleer now. If so, he'll stand up for me."

Russ settled himself into a more comfortable position in preparation for sleep.

Caloon spoke again. "Are you sure you want to go that far with me? Better think that over very carefully. You might want to ride on across the Kofas, turn west, and travel straight to California. I've heard tell San Francisco is one hell of a town to visit."

One of the horses tossed his head and snorted. Both men turned their heads to look at the disturbance. The animal stood with his ears thrust forward, looking down as if there was something in the grass not to his liking. He walked off a few paces and began to graze again.

Russ did not answer Caloon's question. He closed his eyes and slept.

Something touched Russ's shoulder and his hand leaped for his pistol.

"Easy, Russ. It's just Caloon. It's about two hours 'til dark. Let's ride along a little and find a safer place to make camp for the night. Good water like this might draw some people we don't want to meet."

Russ stood up, holstered his gun, and stretched. The sun hung low in the western sky, a golden ball barely a finger's width above the horizon. The air was less hot and the cottonwoods no longer rained down their mist.

The two men walked toward the horses, kicking up a flurry of grasshoppers that flapped away with a noisy chatter of dry wings.

"Still planning to go into the Kofas with me to join Raasleer's gang?" asked Caloon as they finished saddling the horses.

"I guess so. I don't plan to leave the Territory," answered Russ shortly as he coiled the last rope and swung into the saddle.

"Do you have any money?"

"Only a couple of dollars."

"I'll give you one of those fifty-dollar gold pieces those Indians had if you want to change your mind," said Caloon without looking at Russ. "That would tide you over until you find an honest job if you want to try. You don't have to make up your mind right now. You'll have a couple of days to think it over. It'll take that long for us to find that rustler gang.''

Russ said nothing. He reined his horse out of meadow and rode into the desert brush.

Russ and Caloon rode steadily and had covered nearly ten miles before the dark forced them to halt. The valley had narrowed down and low rolling hills surrounded them. The distant Kofas could no longer be seen, hidden by the darkness.

They found a patch of sandy soil at the base of a tall sloping rock outcrop and, figuring it would make a soft bed, made camp. It was a dry camp with no water for the horses and only the canteens for the men. They hobbled the front legs of the animals and turned them loose to graze.

In the darkness they ate beef jerky and dried fruit taken from the packs of the dead marshals. They did not talk, sitting silently together, looking out across the desert and chewing the tough food. The dry grass rustled softly in the faint evening breeze. Now and then the thump of a horse's hoof came to them as the animal hopped about on tied legs, searching for forage.

Russ spread his blankets and lay down. He stared upward at the stars hanging like bright pricks of light against the velvety blackness of the sky. As he watched, the sky grew lighter and the weaker stars faded. He rolled his head to look to the east and saw the moon, like a half disk of silver, sail up from the darkness below the horizon.

"Caloon, how do men like us, outlaws and killers, finish out their lives?" asked Russ.

Silence stretched for a long moment and Russ decided the man was not going to answer. He closed his eyes and prepared for sleep.

"They die early, violently, and among strangers," Caloon finally answered, his voice cold and flinty.

Russ was surprised at the harshness of the reply. But he knew the man spoke the truth.

"Caloon, would you let me carry one of the gold pieces? You know, just in case."

"Sure," said Caloon and dug one out of his pocket. "Here." He extended his hand out through the half darkness toward Russ. "If you decide to leave, you don't have to say anything. Just ride out. I'll understand. If you're not here in the morning, that might be the best thing you ever did."

Chapter 7

Caloon woke before dawn and raised up to sit on his blanket. He moved slowly and quietly so as not to wake his new comrade. The moon had already flown its arc through the heavens and, continuing its plunging fall to the west, now hid behind the looming bulk of the Kofa Mountains. The stars seemed more than normally distant, providing little light, and the land lay in pitch-black night.

Russ's breathing, low and strong, came from the darkness nearby. Caloon knew the young man's luck was bad; not quite a man yet, his life was aimed down the hard, vicious life of the outlaw. But that path had been chosen by Russ through his own action. Caloon shrugged his shoulders. Russ's past was his own fault, the future his own responsibility.

The rhythm of Russ's breathing subtly changed, increasing slightly. Then the volume faded and Caloon could no longer hear it. He knew with certainty Russ was awake, that somehow even though asleep he had received a signal of danger and was now roused and alert.

Barely audible, muffled by Russ's blankets and probably

also by his hand, Caloon heard the click of the six-gun being cocked. Caloon smiled and nodded in the blackness. With his keen reflexes Russ might survive for a short time in this dangerous world. Maybe just for a little while.

Caloon remembered the strength of the young man's hands on his neck. Even half drowned, the man's grip had been strong. The outcome of that struggle might have ended differently had the fight started fairly. But few fights start fairly, and any man who expected it to happen that way was a fool.

Caloon spoke to his unseen companion. "It'll be daylight in an hour. It's always best to leave camp in the darkness in case some enemy has found you and is lying in wait to kill you at first light. So do you want to get an early start?"

"Yes. Sounds right to me," said Russ in a wide-awake voice.

They rolled their blankets and then stood looking out into the night, listening for the horses to move, giving away their location. But the land was silent; even the night insects rested voicelessly.

"The horses must have wandered off or are sleeping," said Russ. He whistled a low-toned note between his teeth. Instantly a friendly answering nicker floated up the hill to them on the night breeze.

"That's my roan," said Russ.

Caloon felt Russ leave, treading noiselessly. A minute or so later his voice called out of the night, "All of them are here. I'll bring them up."

Russ led the three animals near the pile of gear, and he and Caloon began to saddle.

"We'll pick a trail just above where the foothills meet the steeper side of the mountains," said Caloon. "That way we can see for a long distance behind us and have a better chance of seeing anyone following. Should also be more likely to find water up there."

"It'll be cooler up higher, too," said Russ. "But do you expect anybody to be on our tracks so quick?"

"No, and if we stay in the rough country we'll be less apt to run across riders we don't want to see. We should take a great deal of trouble to hide our trail from here on 'cause we don't want to lead a marshal or Indian tracker to Raasleer."

Russ tossed Caloon's and his extra gear up on the back of the third horse and tied it into place. "I'm ready to go," he called.

They rode at a slow pace, letting their mounts pick the way through the brush and rock with their night-seeing eyes. From time to time, the men reined the horses into the hill, forcing them gradually to climb as they progressed across the slope.

The tops of the first range of foothills were reached and the horses stopped on their own volition at the very crest to blow and catch their wind after the long, hard climb. The riders sat watching the morning sun burst forth in brilliant orange above the eastern horizon. A ray of sunlight found the peak of the mountain and began to inch downward toward them.

"No wind and no clouds. Going to be another scorcher," observed Russ.

Caloon did not answer. He twisted around with a squeak of saddle leather to look south across the broad Palomas Plain still filled with gray dawn shadows. Hidden beneath the dark shadows and more than thirty miles away lay the Gila River, and the bodies of four men he and Russ had killed.

Caloon turned back to the front, dismissing the past, and swung his hand to encompass the great bulk of the Kofa Mountains rearing above them to the north and west. "All of that is Raasleer's domain. Counting the Kofas and the smaller mountain range nearby, it must be sixty miles across. Some of the roughest and most godforsaken land in

the Arizona Territory. There's a thousand secret places for
an outlaw gang to hide. And dozens of springs and canyons
to hold the cattle they steal."

Russ measured the vastness of the lava mountains,
marveling at their stark beauty as the sunlight flooded the
towering peaks. He surveyed the terrain carefully, knowing
if he was to survive he must quickly learn the trails that
penetrated this immense land and the location of every
water hole.

Three distinct ranges of foothills stepped up to the final
rampart of the mountains. On the higher hills patches of
dark green juniper lay scattered about. Three thousand feet
above that, ponderosa pine clothed the mountain slopes,
growing especially dense in the moist coves where snow
was piled in tremendous drifts by the frigid winter winds.
And finally, towering above all the lesser land, the ultimate
crown of the mountain, Polaris Peak, its soaring rock spires
dominating everything.

"What mountain is that over there about fifteen miles and
the one beyond that about twice as far away?" asked Russ,
pointing east.

"That's the Eagletails in the far distance. The closer
mountains are the Little Horns. Raasleer uses both of them
sometimes to hide stolen cattle in. But the Kofas are much
bigger and have more live water so he keeps most of his
cattle there. At least that's what Tanwell told me."

"Why hasn't someone gone into the Kofas to catch
Raasleer?"

"Several posses have tried to hunt him down. All they
got for their effort was sore asses and now and then a
warning bullet from some great distance or from a high-rim
rock that only a crow could get up to. Those posses have
found some cattle at times and took them away with them."

Caloon took off his hat and wiped the sweat from his
forehead. "It'd take an army to get Raasleer out of those

mountains and he's not worth that much yet. But as much trouble as he is causing, the Army will come one of these fine days. Maybe this fall before he starts his cattle drive to Mexico. Or they may wait for him down in the desert and try to catch him while he is driving them south. I would expect that to be the plan most likely to succeed."

"Seems like Raasleer's a king with a fortress and as long as he stays in it he'll be safe," said Russ.

"You won't find it to be anything like that. It's not a castle. The mountain is a place where outlaws hide and live a hard life. Let's ride on."

The hot fireball of the sun climbed its heavenly arc, passed the zenith, and began to fall toward the peak of the mountain. The men met no other riders and saw no sign of cattle. Nor did they find any water.

Toward mid-afternoon, they spooked a band of wild mustangs, blacks and browns, on a projecting point of the mountain. The herd stallion, a powerful black with many battle scars, had seen the men before they spotted him. His nostrils quivered and sucked at the air, and his large intelligent eyes watched every move of the intruders.

As the men drew near, he bugled his challenge at them. He charged his harem of mares and their colts, his ears laid back and his teeth showing, pushing them before him around the side of the mountain toward a large thicket of juniper and safety.

As the band streaked through the juniper, the black animal bugled again, threateningly, encouraging the laggards to hurry, to give their all to escape. A colt tumbled, falling hard, his long legs thrashing the air. Then he was up and racing away, his little lungs pumping. The large bruise on his shoulder from his fall was unfelt in his fear.

"If we had time, we could backtrack that herd and find their water hole," said Caloon.

"Don't we have all the time in the world?" asked Russ.

"No, the sooner we get to working with Raasleer, the larger our share of this year's stolen cattle will be. I'm sure he has several herds of cattle already hidden in the mountains now. There're several weeks left before the first snow falls and he'll rustle some more before they're driven south for sale to the Mexicans. We got to help him rustle these last bunches and make the drive to Mexico."

"All right," said Russ. "The horses can do without water until tomorrow, if we don't luck out and find some before that."

Shortly after noon, when the heat was at its greatest and the horses were lathered with sweat, the men stopped beneath a rock cliff. They rode their mounts in under the lava ledge, loosened the saddles, and lay down to rest in the shade. Occasionally one of the men would get up and walk out to a vantage point and, using Russ's telescope, search along their backtrail for approaching enemies. The route across the desert basin and the hills always lay empty.

Mid-afternoon the two riders again took up their journey, working northwest along the front of the Kofa Mountains. Caloon rode morose and untalking. Russ tried to draw him out with questions about the roads and trails into the mountains. The older man did not respond. With a strange haunted look on his face, he rode stonily in the lead. After several attempts to talk with Caloon, and not understanding the change in the man, Russ gave up.

Caloon knew he had made a great mistake, had unthinkingly encouraged the young man to come with him to join Raasleer's outlaw gang. Caloon feared that once among the owlhoots, caught up in their criminal ways, Russ would never be able to break away and find an honest life among decent men. Sadness filled Caloon; had his son been alive, he would never have allowed the innocent to come with him.

Russ's attention to the details of the landscape did not lag. His restless eyes constantly marked the location of prominent landmarks, filing them away for future reference. Often he cast his glance along their backtrail, not only to look for pursuers, but also to record its appearance from the opposite viewpoint so he could return, even in the dark if necessary.

They selected a dry camp in the late evening on a high knob of the mountain. Russ dismounted and climbed out to the farthest jutting point of rock. He looked down upon the foothills, and beyond in the far distance, and two thousand feet below, the desert valley of the Palomas.

A coyote lay napping in the shade at the base of the rock just below Russ. He was startled awake by the human's sudden noisy appearance and sprang up and loped away.

Russ's hand stabbed for his six-gun, drew, cocked it, and aimed at the coyote in one swift movement. He did not shoot, only followed the moving target with the open end of the barrel. Then he holstered the gun. Practice, always practice, he thought, and do it at unexpected times from strange unnatural positions.

He returned to where Caloon sat near the horses. "How about giving the ponies half a gallon of water each?" asked Russ. "It won't mean much to them, but I think we should do it."

"All right, but save us a full drink for tomorrow morning," agreed Caloon, speaking for the first time in several hours.

Russ poured his hat full from a canteen and held it out for his roan to drink. The thirsty animal, watching him with gold-flecked brown eyes, slurped it up noisily. Russ gave the other horses equal amounts of the scarce water.

The sun sank below the horizon. A breeze found its way around the side of the mountain and began to carry away the heat from the rocks and ground still hot with memories of the burning sun. The night insects crept from their daytime hiding places and those that flew launched themselves into the air to find a place to feed.

The high-frequency cries of the tiny winged life woke the dozing nighthawk. He rose and stretched and waddled to the mouth of his burrow in the rocks of the mountainside. With his unimaginably keen eyesight, he saw the swarm of insects, like a thin mist, rise up from the ground and circle and mill in the sky.

The nighthawk, hungry after his daylong fast, yet knowing he had much time to hunt, paused to groom his wing feathers with his tongue and beak. As he finished cleaning and shaping each feather, it was carefully placed in the exact position for best flight.

With great ease, the hawk lifted up from the land, the white spots on the underside of each wing flashing like tiny beacons. A four-winged bug with a short plump body sailed into the path of the hawk. He scooped the creature from the air, crushed the soft carcass with his bill, tasted the sweet flesh and juice, and then speedily devoured all with one gulp.

At the delicious flavor of the insect, the feeding frenzy surged through the nighthawk. He sounded his killing cry, screaming it loudly, piercing the half darkness for nearly a mile. He finished and dove to catch another bug, instantly flung himself to the right, and caught yet another.

A second nighthawk swooped in, eager to join the attack on the airborne prey. Then a swarm of the voracious birds appeared out of the deepening shadows and with raucous half-hooting calls of delight, united with the first two for the feast.

Russ and Caloon sat and watched the erratic darting acrobatics of the hunting nighthawks and listened to their savage cries.

"That's sure a wild sound," said Russ.

"Yep, wild and hard. Same as the land. All the brush has thorns. A man can wear out a pair of boots in a week, a horse a quarter inch of iron, and when it rains it's a gully washer. But I have seen the desert bloom. One year in every ten to fifteen, a warm spring rain comes and it continues through June and July. Flowers of a thousand colors bloom and cover the land, even growing from the rocks, and the grass is the greenest you ever hope to see. Some of the seeds must have waited for years for just the right weather to make them grow."

Russ did not answer. He had never seen what Caloon described. He let his mind visualize and contemplate that wonderful sight.

Caloon went to his blankets, but Russ remained to watch. Finally the dark obscured his vision; still he sat and listened to the sounds of the night.

He thought of his mother. What was she thinking, doing? Was his father healing rapidly from the bullet wound? Russ hated being separated from them. He was an outcast without a goal in life, completely rudderless. A heavy loneliness crept in to grip his heart.

He wondered what his new life—an outlaw life—would bring. He looked in the direction where Caloon slept. Though the man was strange, his advice to ride on to California was more than likely sound. Russ fingered the gold coin. Maybe tomorrow he would strike out on his own.

"Damn these boots," cursed Caloon, "they're killing my feet."

Russ, his mouth dry and pasty, did not answer.

The two men walked, leading their gaunt, thirsty horses along the rocky side of the main flank of the Kofas. It was early evening of the third day and the sun burned down with the same ferocious heat it had poured on the earth for the past week. They were beyond the easternmost swell of the mountain. The valley of the Palomas lay far behind, and the Ranegras Desert crowded the base of the mountain. They had found no water and all the canteens had been dry since the morning drink.

Caloon led the way across a land that had grown more steep and broken as the two men had worked their way north. They traveled a trail that hung at an elevation that contoured the mountainside just above where the deep cuts of the canyons were birthed. From this vantage point they could see down into the rock-walled trenches that slashed east through the foothills.

Suddenly Caloon halted, ducked down, and backed away from the crest of a small ridge he had just topped. He jerked his horse quickly out of sight. "There's something moving. An animal on the skyline about three hundred yards ahead. Loan me your glasses. Hurry!"

Russ dragged the telescope from a saddlebag and shoved it at Caloon.

The man scrambled back to the ridge line.

"A buck deer, a big one," said Caloon in a voice barely audible. "He's moseyin' down the slope and angling off a little to the north."

He crawled away from the crown of the hill and, grinning widely, walked to where Russ held the horses. "Deer water in the late evening or early night. That buck was taking it slow and easy, and I believe he is on his home range. His water hole will be within a mile or two."

Caloon dropped down on the ground and stretched out his legs. "We've got it made now. We'll wait awhile and then follow that old rascal to the water. Main thing is that we don't scare him and cause him to run off in the wrong direction."

"Let me take a look," said Russ.

The deer, a large gray animal with a tinge of brown draped over his shoulders, nibbled at the tender tips of an occasional bush as he ambled down the slope. He raised his magnificent antlered head—the main beams nearly as large as a man's wrist and with four tines on a side—to scan ahead with cautious eyes. Velvet, dry and peeling, hung in short streamers from the antlers and waved in the wind with each movement of his head.

Russ moved his field of view down the incline, trying to locate the destination of the deer. A ridge cut across a few hundred yards in front of him, obscuring his view.

As the minutes passed, the buck leisurely worked his way behind the hill.

"He's out of sight," said Russ. "We can move up to the next point."

Caloon nodded and, gathering the reins of the horses up in his hand, followed quietly behind Russ down across the swale and partway up the next slope. After tying their mounts, they crept up to the summit. A low quarrelsome bawl of a cow floated to them as they peered over.

A saucer-shaped basin, maybe a mile across, lay before them. In some ancient time, a fracture caused by some powerful force had split the earth, slicing down through the rock layers of a shoulder of the Kofas. Billions of tons of rock and its mantle of soil had slipped four or five hundred feet down the mountainside. The mass had come to rest in almost a horizontal attitude with a shallow depression occupying the center. Above the basin, broken, crumpled beds of rock hung from the ruptured flank of the mountain.

Near the top of the basin, a dark green patch of grass with a few willows marked the location of a moist area. Several reddish-brown cows stood in the meadow with their heads down, grazing.

"Cows mean humans are close," said Russ. "What should we do?"

Caloon stepped astride his horse. "We came for water so

let's go get it. If someone shoots at us, ride like hell back the way we came."

Russ mounted and spurred his mount to catch up with Caloon and take up position on the man's right. He pulled his rifle and held it ready in front of him across the saddle.

The cow was quiet now and the basin lay silent under the hot sun. The muted thud of the horses' hooves and an occasional creak of leather were the only noises.

The buck deer spotted the two riders when they appeared on the ridge top. He froze, filled with alarm. He thrust his ears forward, listening intently, and watched them ride into his basin.

"There he goes," exclaimed Russ, pointing at the great stag as it bolted away toward the low end of the valley.

The frightened animal raced through a herd of a dozen cows, frightening the clumsy animals into awkward, galloping flight for a few hundred feet before they stopped. They milled about, their tails switching nervously and their ears cupped in the direction of the riders.

The deer sped directly for a narrow canyon that drained the basin on the east side. With a long, easy bound he leaped a rock fence that blocked the mouth of the canyon, and continued at full tilt down the dry stream bed.

Caloon gave only the slightest glance at the deer. His attention was riveted on the cows, interpreting the variety of brands. He spoke in a low voice. "The cows look like stolen stock to me. I count three different brands. I bet Raasleer rustled them and has temporarily cached them here."

"Maybe we've accomplished two things, found water and Raasleer," said Russ.

"I don't think Raasleer would be caught near a herd of stolen cattle. He's too savvy for that. But somebody else may be watching the cows. If so, that thick patch of mountain mahogany on the far side of the valley is the most likely place for them to be hiding."

"There really isn't any need for anybody to hang around except to see that the cows have water," said Russ. He pointed to the place where the deer had vanished. "They were probably driven in by way of that canyon that leads off toward the low country, and then the gap closed by the rock fence. The cows can't go back home that way even if they tried and now they're anchored to the water here in the valley as tightly as if they were tied with long lassos. They'll graze out a mile or two, then come back here to drink every day."

"Yep. You're right. Maybe there's no one here. Let's just ride straight up to the spring. Don't pay any attention to the cows."

They crossed the open land to the willows near the water. The spring was weakly oozing a small flow of water from a mucky quagmire of cow tracks and manure. Two cows lifted their muddy noses up from where they had been sucking at the slow seep of water and trotted off with a bawl of protest at being disturbed.

"The spring needs to be dug out if it's going to water the number of cows that're here," said Russ.

"They can use the hole we dig," said Caloon. "Begin work up at the head of the flow just below that thin rock ledge until we get clean water. Help me keep watch while we dig so someone can't sneak up on us without us seeing them."

Gouging at the muck with broken lengths of willows and scooping out the slimy soil with their hands, the two men sought the source of the water. Finally a depression big as a washtub had been excavated and the clean, cool water bubbled up from deep within the earth.

"You drink first," said Caloon, washing the mud from his hands and picking up his rifle. With a worried frown on his face, he swiveled his eyes, sweeping the basin for danger.

Russ lay down and drank deeply, the cool wetness of the water pleasant in his parched mouth. And when he stood up, the cool weight felt comfortable in his gullet.

Caloon killed his thirst while Russ kept lookout. Then they led up the horses to drink their fill with noisy pulls at the water.

Caloon grew more edgy, his skittish eyes darting. Russ sensed the man's tenseness and also turned to survey the brush and boulder fields on the opposite side of the valley.

He felt his short hairs curl. "Somebody is watching," he said in a tight voice. "I don't know where they are, but they're here."

"You're right," answered Caloon. "The rustlers are here and looking at us over the sights of rifle barrels. Get ready to ride." He mounted quickly.

"Hold up half a minute," said Caloon, "I'm going to make one try to get them to show themselves."

He called out in a full-mouthed voice that rolled loudly over the basin. "Hello, whoever you are. I know you're there and I want to talk. We mean no harm."

The cows hastily raised their heads from the grass and looked at the men. But there was no answer to Caloon's proposal.

"Hellooo! We want to talk!" Caloon called again.

There was no answer.

"Goddamn them. They're someplace close," Caloon cursed. "If we could get them to show themselves and talk, we might find out where Raasleer is holed up."

Caloon waited a brief moment before a reply. Then he spoke to Russ. "Let's get out of here before they start shooting. Ride at a normal pace and hope they don't get excited or think we're afraid. They may be like dogs that attack anything that runs from them."

Chapter 8

━━━━━━━━━━━━━━━━━━━

The natural barrier of lava rock, and the treacherous slopes of talus precariously balanced against its sides, blocked Russ and Caloon's route to the north. The obstacle had been encountered shortly after they had left the basin with the stolen cattle. They sat their horses, looking up across the flank of the mountain and evaluating the difficulty of the thousand-foot climb to detour around the massive outcropping of black lava rock.

"The ponies can never make it up over that," said Caloon. "They'll fall at that first rocky face and we'll lose them. We must go east and try to find a way out of this broken-up country." They turned and laboriously began to work their way down toward the lower land of the Ranegras Desert.

It was hellish going. Often they were forced to backtrack because of impassable rim rocks and to dismount and search for passageways the horses could navigate down the broken, rocky slopes. The packhorse fell once and rolled on its load. The tired men did not take time to examine the damage.

"Nothing we can do about whatever is broken," said Caloon disgustedly.

By the time they had reached the desert plain, the daylight had drained from the sky, spilling over the western horizon, leaving a black sky speckled with stars. They made camp where the darkness caught them.

The parched land grew no grass to feed the horses, so the men did not hobble the animals; instead they stretched a picket rope between two mesquite bushes and tethered the mounts to it.

"Bad way to treat the horses, keeping them short of water and no feed," said Russ.

Caloon merely grunted. He stumbled away carrying his blanket and saddlebags. Russ heard him kicking the humps off the ground and his sigh as he lay down. Russ smiled wearily; Caloon was worn out, maybe more so than he was.

Russ made his own bed. Exhausted, both men slept, one lonely saguaro cactus standing silent sentry over them.

They found water near noon the following day and continued for two sun-baked days to the north, searching for the outlaw camp.

"Hell, it may take us all summer to find Raasleer's hideout," said Caloon, glancing at Russ, who rode on his right. "We've poked into dozens of canyons and haven't found any sign at all."

"You said lawmen couldn't find him and now we know why," Russ responded.

"Raasleer will learn of us soon if he doesn't already know. It would be safest for us if we find him first. He's a cagey old fox who doesn't make mistakes. He may shoot us without asking what we want."

They rode the heat of the day, the harsh sunlight hammering their eyes down to a squint. In mid-afternoon they pulled their mounts to a halt as they spotted tracks on

the ground. Caloon chuckled as he looked down at the fresh
horse sign, two sets of shod hooves cutting across in front of
them at a right angle. "Well, look at that now. Fresh, made
this morning."

Russ scanned back along the backtrail of the strange
horsemen. "Coming straight in from the east. Maybe all the
way from Tucson. Do you think some of Raasleer's men
might be returning to camp?"

"This is the first sign of riders we've seen, so it could be,
or it could be Raasleer himself. Let's just tag along and find
out."

Russ and Caloon turned toward the mountain, following
the trail easily. Often they surveyed the land ahead, hoping
for a sight of the two horsemen.

They entered a narrow valley and dogged the trail along a
dry stream that meandered between low brush-covered
hills. The slopes gradually crowded in, changing to steep
vertical rock walls thirty feet or so tall and so close together
the men could barely ride abreast.

The mustangs waded the superhot air. The men sweated
and drank the last of the water from the canteens. The day
grew old, the light faded toward dusk, and long shadows
grew.

"There's a man in the rocks on the right," said Russ in a
low voice. "About sixty yards away at the base of that tall
pinnacle rock. In the shadow. See him?"

"I see him. We may have found them at last," muttered
Caloon. "Don't move suddenly or touch your gun. I'll do
the talking." Caloon reined his horse to face the lookout
and held up his hand palm outward in greeting.

"We're looking for Raasleer," he called to the guard
standing motionless, ready with his rifle near his shoulder.

The man remained silent and unmoving.

"Raasleer?" called Caloon again, raising his voice in a

question. "We're looking for Raasleer. We're friends. Is he here?"

In the dark shadows beneath the wide brim of his hat, the face of the man was hidden. He shifted a large cud of tobacco into his cheek, and spat a stream of tobacco juice to clear his mouth, but did not speak. He stabbed up the canyon with the barrel of his rifle without removing his watchful eyes from Caloon or Russ.

"Talkative son of a bitch," muttered Caloon. He pulled his mount back to the front and kicked him ahead, iron shoes clattering noisily against the rocks in the bottom of the wash.

"Do you think there will be other guards before we find the hideout?" questioned Russ.

"I would guess one more. The canyon is too narrow here, too dangerous to make a camp. And there's no water. One man on top of the rocks could trap and hold several men. The camp will be up there where the land is open and the air cooler." Caloon pointed ahead and up toward the higher elevation.

"From those high points they can see for miles and hear a signal from the lookouts. If the law or a bunch of ranchers tried to slip up on the rustlers they would simply scatter and ride out to safety. Remember, Raasleer has been stealing cattle here for nearly six years. He knows this land better than any man. Only the eagles might know it better and that's doubtful."

They rode steadily ahead, the canyon becoming deeper, a narrow defile that caught no sun. The tracks of the two horsemen they followed were invisible most of the time, showing only on the small sandbars created by the water where it had eddied.

Russ saw dead float wood and other flood trash wedged into cracks and crevices of the rocks higher than he could reach from horseback. Pointing at the broken and splintered chunks of wood that showed the flood height of the stream, Russ spoke to Caloon. "Sure wouldn't want to get caught in here in a cloudburst. There's no way we could get out alive."

"Don't talk," commanded Caloon sharply, "just watch and stay alert. If trouble starts, get your gun out fast and help me. If Tanwell ain't here, we may have to shoot our way out. And that'll be damn tough to do."

Russ almost snapped back in anger at the order, but he caught himself, remembering how off guard he had been when Caloon had killed the Indians.

The rock, half as big as a man's head, zoomed down from above, hit with a crash, and bounced with a rattle of gravel across the trail in front of them. Russ and Caloon jerked their horses in and threw their eyes upward.

A big man with a long bristly beard stared down from the overhanging rock wall.

"I could've shot both of you with my eyes shut," said the man crouched hardly a dozen yards away.

Caloon nodded in agreement with the statement. "I believe that. The other lookout saw us, too, but we ride in the open for a reason. We wanted to be seen to show we mean no harm. We're looking for Raasleer and a man named Tanwell."

"So why tell me?" growled the man, stepping back from the lip of the overhanging rock and moving his rifle to point more directly at the two riders below.

Russ sensed the minute shift of Caloon in preparation to draw his own pistol and shoot. He quickly measured his own angle of fire up to the man on the rock. When Russ saw the man intently watching Caloon, he slipped his hand an inch closer to the butt of his six-gun and waited for the fight to begin.

"Young man, don't play me for a blind fool," snapped the man in a deadly voice. "If you move your hand a fraction more toward your gun, I'm going to blow your face away."

Russ was startled. The man still appeared to have his eyes riveted on Caloon, but he had seen that small movement of Russ's hand. These men lived by their wits and reflexes and would not be tricked.

The man swung his full stare upon Russ. In the lessening daylight the eyes bore down emotionless as a snake.

"You can ride on in and look for this *hombre*, Raasleer," said the man, "but I doubt if you will be riding out."

They heard a shrill whistle behind them as they left. The man was signaling their approach ahead.

They found the camp of the rustlers on the narrow bench where an acre or so of juniper bordered a small stream running down from the high reaches of the Kofas. Five men sat talking in the shade.

"We'll go in slow," said Caloon. "If things go wrong, start shooting and ride your horse straight over them. Kill as many as you can and as fast as you can."

The outlaws stood up and watched Russ and Caloon approach. A tall, rail-thin man said something and the other members of the gang fanned out to flank him on each side.

"Raasleer's in the middle," said Caloon from the side of his mouth. "Tanwell told me what he looks like. He's mine if it comes to a fight."

Not a word was uttered as the two riders drew rein and sat facing the outlaws. Caloon and Russ made no effort to dismount.

Raasleer sized up the big blond man and the younger, almost boyish, rider beside him. He detected no fear in either. The older man appeared nonchalant, his head cocked to the side at a cynical angle. But the youth's hands were nervous.

"If you're lost, that's too bad," said the outlaw leader.

Caloon surveyed the opposition and searched for Tanwell. He found all the men strangers. Without Tanwell to back up his word, Russ and he were in a mighty tight fix.

Caloon swung his eyes back to Raasleer and grinned without mirth. With his left hand he pointed to the east and then to the west. "That's to Tucson and that's to California, so you see we ain't lost. We're looking for Raasleer and I think we have found him."

"What makes you think I'm Raasleer?" asked the man.

"A fellow I knew in Yuma Pen once told me that Raasleer was a tall skinny *hombre* that if you took his boots off could be used to swab out a shotgun barrel."

Raasleer's face flashed hard and his mouth clamped tightly shut. His eyes squinted nearly shut as if sighting down a gun barrel. One of the outlaws beside him snickered shortly.

Russ's pulse jumped at Caloon's response. It was an insult and the man's laugh made it much worse. Why badger the bandit leader? What was to be gained?

Caloon continued to speak. "My name is Caloon and I just broke out of Yuma, that new little palace built on Dome Mountain. Tanwell can vouch for me. I need a job, one that will make me some good money."

Raasleer remained silent, his angry eyes studying the convict. Russ could see the man's rapid assessment of the possible actions to take against Caloon. Russ hoped it would not be to signal the outlaw pack to attack.

Raasleer finally spoke. "We don't need any gun hands. But we can always use three good horses. Banty over there, his horse stepped in a crack in the rock and broke its leg, so he's down to one horse. I want all my men to have two horses apiece. So why don't you and your sidekick step down and we'll take the horses off your hands."

Caloon laughed, sharp and brittle. "I guess not. What would me and my partner ride?"

"Dead men don't need horses," said Raasleer.

Russ felt the tension flash like lightning through all the men. The name of the game had been called. His muscles grew taut, ready to jab the spurs into the flank of his horse, drive it straight into the outlaws, ride the sons of bitches down. And he would shoot Banty and the man next to him as he rode through.

But it was at least ten jumps of his horse to the protection of the juniper. And many guns would be firing at him at close range.

Rocks rattled on the slope above the camp and a horseman swooped down the steep trail and into camp. He quickly saw and interpreted the face-off, the threatening posture that meant gunplay ready to explode. He drew fast rein on his mount.

"Crazy Caloon," called the strident voice of the new arrival, "don't draw on Raasleer for he'll surely kill you."

Caloon kept his eyes tied to Raasleer's. "Well, I'm sure as hell not wanting to die yet," he said. He was not certain Raasleer could actually beat him in a showdown, but he wanted to join up with the outlaw, not fight him.

Tanwell rode up closer.

"Crazy, I thought you still had time to do before you got turned loose out of Yuma Pen."

Caloon slowly and deliberately turned away from Raasleer and faced Tanwell. He never had liked the man, but he looked at the thin ferret face and the small restless eyes and grinned. "I took a walk when no one was watching."

"Do tell. That's not an easy thing to do," said Tanwell. "And where are the Quechans? I hope to hell you haven't led them here."

"They're dead down on the bank of the Gila. Seems they had a little accident and stopped some .45-caliber lead."

Caloon shoved his hat to the back of his head. "I remembered you talking about Raasleer being one damn good rustler, so I came to join up."

Tanwell dismounted. "Well, I guess he is. I'm making money or will be when we drive some cattle into Mexico. Let me introduce you two formal-like."

Tanwell walked between the men. "Raasleer, this is Crazy Caloon. Him and me bunked together at Yuma when he was first brought to the pen. He played it wise and stayed out of trouble. I'll vouch for him as a man who knows how to take orders and will do more than his share of the work. He'll not back down from a fight either."

Raasleer, mollified by Tanwell's compliments and Caloon's obvious willingness to back off, replied, "All right, Tanwell, I'll take your word for him. But what's this kid doing here?"

"He's with me," said Caloon. "I'll stand responsible for his actions."

"What's his name?" Raasleer asked Caloon.

"I can speak for myself. My name is Russ."

"Russ what?" asked Raasleer.

"Just Russ. Last names don't mean anything."

"Not to us anyway," said Raasleer. "Climb down and eat." He stalked away.

The outlaws relaxed and drifted off to gather again around the members who had arrived ahead of Russ and Caloon. Russ heard the mention of Tucson before he and Caloon went to their horses. They unsaddled and turned the animals loose to find the water in the creek.

"The grass is fresh. Looks like the camp is new," observed Russ.

"They probably change camps every few days. It wouldn't be smart to stay long in one place. After a while there would be so many tracks in and out of camp, a posse could follow them in easy."

"Still couldn't capture them in a hideout this well protected."

"The reason Raasleer has survived is not to get trapped where he had to fight a losing battle. Tanwell says he likes money and will take chances to get it, yet he plays it cautious. And I've heard in other places that Raasleer is damn quick and accurate with a handgun."

Russ turned to look at Caloon.

"Then why did you insult him and get him riled up?"

"I'm going to give you a piece of advice on how to act when dealing with a bunch of killers and robbers like every one of these men are. Don't show any fear or weakness or they'll take what is yours and kill you. If they think we're afraid of them, they'll destroy us even with Tanwell vouching for us. Maybe they won't do it immediately, but in some raid or fight they'll put us in the most dangerous position or use us as a decoy while they escape. Now you think about that. When I'm not around, they'll test you. So get ready for it."

"I don't want to fight any of them."

Caloon guffawed deep down in his throat. "We're complete strangers. Unknown. We're not worth a plugged nickel to them. Later, after a couple of raids to rustle cattle and we prove ourselves, they may partway accept us. You're strong. If one of them wants to fight with fists you gouge his eyes out, quick as you can. If it's to be with guns, shoot to kill. If you don't give all the signs you won't take any bullshit and will fight, you won't last out the summer."

"You mean just stand up and shoot at each other without any reason?"

"Oh, they'll give you a reason," said Caloon. "Let's find a camp away from the others and near the horses. How about that clump of junipers near the picket rope?"

"All right by me."

Caloon picked up his saddle, bedroll, and rifle and

walked into the grove of trees to pile the gear on the ground. He continued toward the cooking pot, squatting over a small smokeless fire.

Russ remained standing near the horses and watched Caloon go up to the fire. The escaped prisoner knelt and, pulling a belt knife taken from the dead marshal, cut a thick steak from a haunch of beef hanging from a low limb of a juniper. He tossed the meat into a skillet and placed it on the fire to cook. While he waited, he took a tin plate from a stack of them on the ground and dipped out a ladle of something from the pot and began to eat.

Russ was ravenous for food, but instead of joining Caloon he tore off a handful of coarse grass and walked to his horse, which was drinking from the stream. The animal turned his head to identify the approaching man. Russ gently stroked the long head, rubbing the bony jaw, glad of the familiarity of the horse. He began to work at the rubdown, beginning the cleaning massage at the muscular shoulder.

He needed time to think, to get his mind in order as to what was right and what was wrong in an outlaw camp. What response should he make to what action or event? Caloon had told him to maim or kill quickly any man who threatened him. Could he do that? He had shot the two lawmen to save his father, but he did not want to kill again.

Russ finished the rubdown of his horse and did the same for Caloon's and the spare. Soothed by the accustomed work and satisfied he had a reasonable grasp of the true danger in the new situation, he joined Caloon and began to prepare his own supper.

The discussion between the members of the gang and those who had come in from Tucson came to an end. The men spread a blanket, a deck of cards was dug from someone's gear, and a game of poker began.

Tanwell strode up to where Caloon and Russ sat under a

juniper. He dropped down on the mat of needles covering the ground and stretched out his legs.

"What's the setup here, Tanwell? How many men does Raasleer have?"

"Ten at the moment."

"I only see five, six counting you. And we saw two on lookout. Where are the others?"

"One is out riding the circuit, keeping the cattle bunched and the springs dug out to water the cows. One is off scouting an Englishman who is starting a big cattle operation over at Gila Bend."

"Seems like an Englishman would be lost in the Arizona Territory."

"Not this one. He's partner of an old wolf of a rancher named Blackaby. Also, he's hired some of the best cowboys in the Territory to ride for him. It appears he has plenty of money. Anyway, this fellow and Blackaby have bought out four or five small ranchers along the Gila to get their irrigated meadows. Just recently they've brought in a couple thousand head of cattle. The word is the Englishman's going to build himself a mansion on the south end of the Gila Bend Mountains. When he calls in his hands to help build the house, Raasleer plans to hit his herd, take two hundred head or so, and push them to Mexico for some quick money."

"I remember you telling me he always made one big drive in the fall. How come he's doing this different?"

"Yeah. You remember right. He steals a few cows from several ranches, takes them from the range farthest from the headquarters and where no one will miss them until fall roundup. Even then the cattlemen most often don't know if they've been stolen or just lost, or maybe killed by wolves. A natural loss is normal. Raasleer bunches the stock, then drives south and has them sold in Mexico before anyone knows.

"But some of us are broke. Those men over there are playing for pennies. We've talked Raasleer into making a quick trip south. We need supplies"—Tanwell grinned crookedly—"but most of all we need to get some whiskey and some women."

"He might be making a mistake to change a winning plan," said Caloon. "Who are the best gunhands?"

"Raasleer is the best, but a close second is Kanttner. You must have seen him; he's one of the lookouts today. Big man with a beard."

"Yeah. We saw him. What is the name of the second lookout?"

"That would be Pratt. Smart aleck type of bastard. Always pulling tricks on somebody. Now, probably the next best gun is Berdugo, that little Mex sitting over there playing poker. Also, without a doubt, he is the best man with a knife. Keeps a throwing blade strapped between his shoulders. The other men are all good, just a notch below the three I mentioned. Raasleer won't keep a man who's a coward or can't use a gun good. But Raasleer's mean and got the bluff on everybody."

"Anything special about the others?"

"No," said Tanwell, looking at the card players. "Banty's the little man sitting with his back to us. Gredler is the square-built man on the right. Jones is opposite him. A man named Lewett is out riding the herds."

"Who's the next boss after Raasleer?"

"That'd be Corddry, the one that is at Gila Bend. He's a back shooter, so watch him."

"What's the news from Tucson?" asked Caloon.

"The word of your escape hasn't reached town yet. If it had, it might've gone easier for you. It's lucky I happened to ride in when I did."

Caloon nodded in agreement. "What else?"

"Tucson is paying the salaries of two deputy marshals.

Tough men, the story is, and fast with their guns. The town council is fed up with the robbery, rustling, and killing going on. The fellows that just came in did not get a chance to see the deputies. Seems they're out chasing some jayhawk that has been pulling off robberies round about for several years."

Raasleer stalked up and looked down at the three men sitting on the ground.

Caloon ignored the presence of the outlaw leader and spoke to Tanwell. "Lot of those types of fellows in the Territory."

Raasleer spoke. "I see Tanwell has told you of the marshals. They're trailing someone out this way someplace. Did you see sign of them?"

Caloon glanced at Russ for a few seconds, and then stood up, arched his chest, and pointed to his shirt. On the cloth over his heart was a less faded spot, darker than the surrounding material. "Look at this. What shape can you make out?"

Tanwell, a puzzled expression on his face, arose and moved in close to examine the blurred outline indicated by Caloon.

"Goddamn!" exclaimed Tanwell. "Looks like the outline of a lawman's badge."

"And here's the badge," said Caloon, pulling the shiny metal object from his pocket. "I happened to run into the two marshals on the Gila four days ago." He chuckled coldly. "I buried them there." He laughed again, staring straight into Raasleer's eyes.

Raasleer's eyes locked with Caloon's. Russ felt the challenge spark between the two men.

"Goddamn, Crazy, you killed . . ." Tanwell started to speak.

Caloon reached out swiftly with his big hands and grabbed Tanwell by the shirt front and jerked him up close.

"Tanwell, you call me Crazy one more time and I'll shoot you," hissed Caloon, his angry eyes stabbing into Tanwell's startled face.

Tanwell tried to pull free, but Caloon tightened his grip, the cloth of the shirt tearing. And Caloon shook the smaller man, snapping his head back and forth on his spindly neck.

"Do you understand? My name is Caloon. Now say it."

"Caloon. Caloon is your name," said the frightened Tanwell in a hoarse whisper.

"Say it out real loud so the rest of the men can hear," ordered Caloon.

"Caloon! Caloon! Caloon!" shouted Tanwell.

"That's good," said Caloon, releasing Tanwell and spinning about to stare at the other gang members. He let his challenging eyes dwell on each man, warning them to beware. They glared back, their hostility not masked.

Caloon stopped his eyes on Raasleer. "I'll do more work than any man you got. And Russ will do his share. We want a full share, same as the others."

"Like hell a full share," snorted Raasleer. "The summer and the work for this year is half over. We already have six hundred cows stashed away. But there are more cows to rustle and a drive to make to Mexico. I'll give each of you one half share."

"How many shares do you take?" questioned Caloon.

"Three shares, and Corddry takes two."

Caloon turned to face Russ. "What say, partner, to the offer?"

"I'd say that is a fair offer," answered Russ, hoping the violence would go no further.

"We'll take the half share," said Caloon.

With one terse nod of his head, Raasleer turned and stalked away. I will give you payment for your work, he thought, if you live long enough to collect it.

Chapter 9

∙∙∙∙∙∙∙∙∙∙∙∙∙∙∙∙∙∙∙∙∙∙∙∙∙∙∙∙∙∙∙∙∙

Raasleer called Caloon from his blankets at daybreak. Russ had heard the gang leader's approach, and lay listening to the man's orders to Caloon.

"Go up the mountainside a mile or so to that big spur of rock facing east. That's about two thousand feet above us here and you can see for miles. Out to the southeast and setting off by itself fifteen miles or so is one single-peaked mountain. It's called Turtleback, if you are familiar with it.

"Now the Englishman, sooner or later, is going to call his range riders in to help build the new house. Corddry is to let us know when that happens. Instead of him riding all the way back here, he'll signal from the top of Turtleback with a big smoky fire. Watch for it. Soon as we see the smoke we leave to join up with him. That way we can save several hours riding time. Take a telescope. You got one?"

"Russ has one I can borrow," said Caloon. He saddled and left immediately, following the exact trail Tanwell had used the day before.

Russ arose leisurely and bathed in the stream. As he dried himself, one of the outlaws, identified by Tanwell as Jones, passed close by on horseback. The man did not speak. He touched spurs to his mount and left at a fast gallop to the west.

Shortly thereafter, Gredler and Banty rode off down the canyon. Half an hour later Kanttner and Pratt, having been relieved from lookout, came in, had a bite to eat, and flopped down on their blankets under a juniper.

When the sun was high enough not to bother his view to the east, Russ climbed the flank of the mountain to a location from where he could see a great distance. For more than two hours he minutely surveyed the mountains, valleys, and streams, imbedding their location and distances in his memory.

Russ saw a horseman come into camp from the north at mid-morning, and judged the man would be Lewett, the one making the inspection trip to check the condition of the rustled cattle in their hidden valleys. Well-run, orderly outfit, thought Russ.

The sun climbed, and burned down from a cloudless sky, baking the mountainside. Yet Russ felt reluctant to go down to the camp. And he realized why he was hesitant. Caloon would not be there. He silently cursed himself and got hastily to his feet to stomp down the slope in the direction of Raasleer and the other bandits. He must not become dependent on Caloon.

Caloon returned late in the day and rode up to dismount near Raasleer. The leader sat under a large juniper on a knob of ground a hundred feet or so distant from where the gang ate and part of them slept.

"No sign of smoke," said Caloon. "I stayed until the shadows of the Kofas covered Turtleback Mountain."

"All right. We'll watch for Corddry's signal again tomorrow. Tell your pard to go up at daylight."

"He'll be there at first light," Caloon answered and walked away, leading his horse toward the stream.

It had been a long dry day and Caloon knelt to drink deeply of the stream. The horse plunged its nose into the cool water and man and animal slaked their thirst.

Feeling refreshed, Caloon led his mount to the picket rope, a lariat stretched tautly between two junipers near a rock outcrop where the base of the mountain met the bench. He slipped the bit from the animal's mouth and stepped up to the rope to tie the reins.

Without warning, the animal lunged upon Caloon, striking him with its head and chest. The man was rammed forward, tripped over the low-hung rope, and fell heavily upon a jumble of rocks. He scrambled up hurt and angry, and whirled about, ready to clout the horse in retaliation for the unprovoked attack. But the horse, its eyes rolling wildly and the whites showing, pranced and tugged at the full length of the reins Caloon held firmly.

Caloon recognized the animal's fright and rapidly looked around to see what had caused it. For a brief moment, among the trees, he spied a man hurrying straight away toward the main camp. He could not identify the figure.

Caloon coaxed the horse up to the picket rope and tied it. He rubbed the neck of the tense animal, calming it down.

Russ saw Caloon approaching, his face hard in anger.

"Somebody goosed my horse while I was about to tie him," exploded Caloon. "Damn animal like to stomp me. Did knock me down on the rocks."

Caloon examined Russ's face; there was no surprise there. He turned and looked toward the picket line and the horses, and then in the direction of the camp. "Goddamn! You saw who did it?"

"Yes, I could see him from here. But let it go. We don't want any trouble."

"Let it go. Hell! The man could have caused the horse to cripple me. And more important, if I don't do something about this, the next trick they play will be worse. Like not giving us our share when the cattle are sold. Now who did it?"

"Caloon, don't start a fight. There's no way it can end without a killing. There's six of them in camp right now. Maybe you'll be the one that gets shot."

"I'll worry about that. Now, for the last time, who was it?"

Russ shook his head in the negative.

"If you don't tell me, I'll call the whole damn bunch of them out for a showdown one at a time."

"It was Pratt," said Russ. "But at least catch him out away from the rest of the gang when you face him."

"No! I'm going to do it now! I want every one of the bastards to know I'll not take rawhiding from any man." Caloon stomped off toward the main camp.

Russ hesitated for a moment, then, hitching his six-gun to a ready position, followed after Caloon. They had accepted each other as partners and he must back Caloon all the way, even to a killing. He felt his determination, hard and cold, blunt his fear at the violence soon to come.

Caloon went directly to the pot hanging over the evening cook fire and slopped a dipper of beans onto a plate. Russ stopped about twenty feet to Caloon's left and hurriedly checked the position of all the gang members present.

Pratt sat near Tanwell and Berdugo, talking to them in a low voice. Raasleer rested on some high ground under a juniper ten yards or so behind Caloon. He appeared to be dozing. Kanttner was not in sight. As Russ shifted back to Caloon, Pratt finished talking and Berdugo and Tanwell laughed.

A red flush crept across Caloon's face at the laughter, believing they were enjoying the joke played on him. He stalked up to Pratt and held out the plate of food to him. In a hard voice he spoke. "Here, Pratt, take my supper."

Pratt squinted up at Caloon in cautious surprise. "I've got enough to eat. You keep it."

"No, I want you to have it."

"Why me?"

"I want you to have a full stomach, for I'm going to shoot you right in the gut for goosing my horse into me." Caloon chuckled wickedly and his hostile eyes glistened. "Men die in the worst way when shot in a full gut. They hang on for days hurting to high heaven before they go."

Pratt climbed to his feet, alert, calculating the odds. The challenge was blunt and could not be avoided. But he felt confident; he was many years younger than Caloon and his hand was quick.

Berdugo and Tanwell hastily stood up and went off to Caloon's right. Out of the corner of his eye, Russ saw Raasleer stand up. Where was Kanttner? Russ hoped to hell the man did not suddenly appear.

Tanwell dropped behind Berdugo as they moved out of the line of fire. He turned to face Caloon from the right side and let his hand fall near his tied down pistol. Tanwell's thin mouth twitched as he worked his courage up; maybe Caloon's attention would be so much on Pratt that he could gun him down and get his revenge for the insult that first day.

Russ saw Tanwell stop, but could only see half of the man for Caloon stood partially in the way, blocking his view.

"Pratt, you goosed my horse in the ass." Caloon's voice was sharp, stinging, showing his eagerness to kill. "For that little trick, here's something for you." Caloon hurled the plate of food at Pratt's face.

Pratt dodged with razor-sharp reflexes. His hand dove for the six-gun strapped to his hip.

Caloon drew and fired. And fired a second time, driving Pratt to the ground.

Russ saw Tanwell's hand flash for his six-gun. Without

conscious thought, Russ's fingers flipped his pistol from its holster. In that split second it took his hand to bring the gun up into alignment on Tanwell, Russ's thumb cocked the hammer and the index finger began to squeeze the trigger.

Russ felt the gun buck in his hand, saw Caloon's vest jump with the close passage of the bullet. Saw Tanwell's eyes snap open wide in surprise and pain at the punch of the bullet.

Tanwell slumped, slack and lifeless, to the ground.

Caloon heard the roar of the gun on his left, felt the sting of a bullet across the front of his chest. He pivoted around just in time to see Russ swing his gun to point at the ground in front of Raasleer.

Berdugo shifted his look from the dead Tanwell to Raasleer, watching for the gang leader's signal as to how the fight was to go.

Caloon continued his turn to the left without stopping and brought his six-gun to bear on Berdugo. He would have preferred to be the one covering Raasleer.

The gang leader stared at Russ with measuring eyes and did not move. The young man's draw had been swift, very swift, and the shot had gone straight through Tanwell's heart. That draw had been faster than Caloon's. Raasleer cursed himself silently for misjudging who was the more dangerous man. It was the kid.

Some instinct told Raasleer he had made a major error in not having gunned Caloon and Russ down while they had been fighting Tanwell and Pratt. But the instant that he could have done that was gone.

"Would you draw on me?" asked Raasleer.

"Only if you tried to shoot Caloon or me," responded Russ, carefully controlling a voice that was on the verge of cracking under the strain.

Raasleer held the young man's look, waiting for it to

waver. The seconds passed and the opposing eyes did not blink once.

Kanttner came running in from the juniper. He stopped quickly, swinging his sight over the two dead men and the standoff. He looked at Raasleer.

The rustler leader removed his hand from the butt of his six-gun.

"If I was going to shoot you, you would already be dead," snorted Raasleer. "I'm short two men now and I need you to help rustle cattle."

He pointed at the dead men. "You and Caloon killed them, so you bury them. Give their weapons to Berdugo for the stores."

Russ and Caloon sat on their blankets as the daylight dimmed into dusk. Caloon spoke, breaking the silence for the first time since the shoot-out. "Thanks for saving my hide. That's one I owe you."

"You would have done the same thing for me," responded Russ.

"That was a close shot. Weren't you afraid you would hit me?"

"Yes, but you were a dead man if I didn't nail Tanwell."

There was a glint of satisfaction in Caloon's eyes. "I'm glad you killed that weasel-faced bastard."

"Did I nick you?" asked Russ.

"The bullet burned me a little when it went past." Caloon unbuttoned his shirt and pointed to a red streak marring the white skin of his chest. "It'll heal soon."

"Good," said Russ. He did not feel friendly toward Caloon. "I'll see you later. I'm going for a walk."

Caloon examined Russ's face, saw the eyes strained, the mouth tight, and the muscles bunched along the jaw and said nothing.

Russ turned and walked away into the juniper. He

continued beyond that for a long distance around the side of the mountain. Damn you, Caloon, there wasn't enough reason to provoke a gunfight, Russ thought. You caused me to kill another man. He let his anger run, allowing it to override his fear of what he was becoming. A killer. He knew the boy was burned out of him. He felt the iron in his stomach and didn't like it.

Long after dark, Russ returned and lay down on his bedroll. Caloon heard the slight stirring of the dry juniper needles. Again Caloon felt the strong misgivings for having made the offer for the young man to come with him to join the outlaw gang.

Russ sat on the point of the mountain and watched to the east as a red dawn slowly increased. A complete silence lay over the land, as if the world waited for the sun to rise before it could come alive. Russ remained motionless, listening to the stillness.

Then a puff of the rising morning wind rustled the dry blades of grass and some insect chirped at being disturbed. The spell broken, Russ lifted the telescope and searched through the morning shadow lying heavy in the broad valley below.

The sun crested the curve of the earth and the silhouette of the round dome of Turtleback Mountain became visible. From the top, a tiny gray plume formed, grew, climbing leisurely. Russ swung the telescope aside, waited a moment, then moved it back to the mountain. The image had grown and in the ever increasing sunlight the smoke column was very plain in the spyglass.

He snapped the glass closed in his hand, hurried to his horse, and swiftly rode down to the camp.

"Are you sure it was Corddry's signal?" questioned Raasleer.

"It was there just as you said it would come," answered Russ. "There's no doubt what I saw."

Raasleer turned to face the remainder of the men and called out loudly so all could hear. "Throw that supply pack on a horse and let's ride. Take an extra horse apiece and one for Corddry and the two lookouts. I mean to meet with Corddry and then make it to the bend of the Gila before nightfall. Lewett, you stay here and help Jones take care of the cows. Keep an eye open so we don't ride into a trap when we come back from Mexico."

With a rattle of metal bits, stamp of horses' hooves, and an occasional curse for a beast to stand still, the men saddled swiftly. They divided the spare mounts among themselves and rode off down the canyon.

Kanttner and Banty, obeying the orders that Raasleer called up to them as he passed, followed along the top of the canyon rim until a break was found in the rocks. Then, with a clatter of loose rock falling and dust swirling up on the wind, they forced their ponies down into the bottom.

There was no conversation. The band of heavily armed outlaws strung themselves out along the narrow canyon and spurred into a ground-eating canter.

From the top of Turtleback Mountain, Corddry watched the group of riders approaching across Palomas Valley from a long distance. Shortly before noon, the men drew close to the western foot of the mountain and Corddry rode down to rendezvous with them.

Raasleer and the others with him had stopped at the first steep slope of the mountain and sat in the shade cast by their horses. Corddry came in warily and made no greetings until the presence of Caloon and Russ was explained. His untrusting face flashed anger at the telling of Pratt and Tanwell's deaths.

Caloon stood up, leaned against the shoulder of his horse,

and glared back truculently. Russ also climbed to his feet and, remembering Tanwell's evaluation of Corddry as a back shooter, kept his attention on the gang's *segundo*, second in command. He waited for the man to take a stand on the killing.

"Well, how about the cows?" asked Raasleer impatiently.

Corddry finished sizing up Russ and Caloon and faced Raasleer. "Two hundred prime breeding heifers in a meadow pasture all by themselves. The Englishman just brought them in from Tucson. They'll bring a top price in Mexico. They're in good condition and can travel fast. In two and a half to three days we can have them south of the border."

"Good," said Raasleer. "Any problems? How about the ranch hands?"

"I saw somebody ride out from the direction of the ranch headquarters about noon yesterday and take the two men who had been building fence back with him. But those heifers are valuable stock. They'll be checked every couple of days."

"Any reason to change the plans we talked about before?" questioned Raasleer.

"Nope. Let's leave it the same. I judge we have one day, maybe a day and a half, to get a good head start. That is, if we take the stock tonight and push them all night. Tomorrow morning, too, if they can stand it. Cover twenty, twenty-five miles while it's still cool. Rest during the heat of the day and start out again in the evening."

Raasleer smiled, pleased, and faced the men. "With luck, we'll make it to Mexico without the Englishman ever coming within sight of us. We'll hide our tracks going to the Englishman's spread, but make as much sign as we can once we start with the cows. I want to leave a good trail for the Englishman to follow. We want him after us and not poking around in the mountains and finding the herds we have stashed there."

"Even a blind man could follow two hundred head of stock," observed Caloon.

Raasleer ignored Caloon. "Who knows the Growler Mountains?"

Banty spoke up. "I cut across the south end once ten years or so ago."

"How about the north part of the mountains?"

"Nope. Never been there."

"I trapped some wild mustangs in the Growlers last year," said Russ. "I know them fairly well."

"You know the mountains stretch north-south and that on the far north end there's a steep shoulder sticking out to the west?"

"I been there," said Russ.

"Then do you know where the nearest water is to that piece of the mountain?" questioned Raasleer.

"Well, I found a spring, a big one, on the east side of the mountain, about three miles from the place you're talking about. And there's a seep about four miles west in the bottom of the wash in Growler Valley. I was trailing a band of wild horses and they led me to it. The water is so close to the surface the mustangs could paw the sand and gravel out deep enough with their hooves to drink."

"I see you do know the land. We'll need water for the heifers and our saddle horses about noon tomorrow."

Russ nodded. "A man with a shovel could dig out quite a lot of water in a couple of hours. Easy enough for two hundred head."

"All right, you're the one to go," said Raasleer. "Take the extra horses, except for a couple we'll drag along with us, and ride to the Growlers. Dig out a water hole and then climb up to the top of the tall point I mentioned. Watch for us, but mainly watch for riders chasing our trail. After we've watered the cows sometime near noon tomorrow, you look close at our backtrail and then come down and meet us with the fresh horses. Can you do that?"

"No problem getting that done," said Russ.

Raasleer and Corddry looked at Russ hard for a long moment. "This is damn important," said Raasleer. "I don't want the Englishman close enough when the sun goes down so he can find us in the dark and shoot the hell out of us. And I want all the horses to be there and well rested. Savvy that?"

Raasleer looked from Russ to Caloon. The meaning was clear. Caloon would be a hostage to insure Russ made no mistakes.

"I'll be there with the horses fed, watered, and rested," promised Russ.

"Then be on your way," ordered Raasleer.

Russ took a small quantity of grub from the packhorse and stowed it away in his own saddlebags. When he began to tie the extra mounts nose to tail, Caloon came to help.

As they worked, Caloon spoke, keeping his voice low so the other men could not hear. "If you want to go to California, this is the time. Take all the horses with you. Be careful where you sell them, for I'd bet my last penny all or most are stolen."

Russ measured Caloon's expression, but before he could say anything, Caloon spoke again. "Now don't hold back on my account. I'll find some reason to be out on point when we come up on Growler Wash. If that seep isn't shoveled out neat and full of water, I'll know you won't be there." Caloon chuckled under his breath. "In that case I'll spur my old horse and ride like hell for safer country. Don't worry, they'll never catch me."

"I'll give it some thought," said Russ.

Corddry strode up and stopped near Russ and Caloon.

"What's all the confab all about?" he asked in a harsh voice.

"Caloon was just telling me how to tie the lead ropes so they won't come loose from the horses' tails," said Russ. "I'm ready to leave now." He stepped astride the roan and, trailing the long string of eight horses, struck off to the south at a fast trot.

The remaining outlaws headed due east toward the green meadows in the flood plains of the Gila River.

Chapter 10

Russ pulled the cavalcade of tired horses to a halt and they stood drooping in the heat. He dismounted and knelt to examine the tracks of the unshod mustangs on the sandy ground.

The horses had come out of the west and continued to the east. Russ judged the sign not older than this morning. The ponies were being ridden, for not once did they deviate from a direct course except to detour around a patch of cactus or a clump of greasewood.

He sat back on his haunches and considered his next move. From the lack of shoes on the horses, he believed the riders to be Indians. There were no drag marks on the ground that would mean a travois had been dragged, hauling family possessions. A band of Indians with no women or children meant a raiding party looking for something to steal or a white man to kill. If the eagle-eyed warriors remained in the area, they would surely discover the cattle being driven through the valley.

Russ glanced up to measure the height of the sun in the

afternoon sky. A hand's width of time remained before the sun would touch the horizon.

It was important to know the Indians' location and, if possible, their plans. However, before it grew dark, the water in Growler Wash had to be found and dug out. The horses must have that water for they had been pushed hard for fifty miles or better since leaving the rustler hideout at daybreak.

He mounted and, taking up the lead rope of the front pony, moved off along the imprints on the ground. Where the Indians had separated to make their way through a dense patch of prickly pear cactus, Russ counted six distinct sets of tracks. Such a small band could not take the cows from the outlaws, but they could stampede and scatter them widely across the brush-covered and arroyo-cut land. It was almost certain several would be missed by the white man's roundup. Then the Indians at their leisure would hunt down the lost animals.

Worst of all, such a delay by the rustlers would allow the Englishman to catch up. Then the killing would begin.

Two miles or so later the Indians abruptly turned due south. Russ followed until he was fairly confident he knew their destination. The tracks headed directly toward one of the more gentle slopes, one a horse could climb on the north end of the Growler Mountains. The braves were seeking high ground from which to spy out possible prey crossing the valley.

For several minutes, Russ examined the flank of the mountain that lay a full mile away. Three thousand feet above the desert floor, lava boulders lay strewn over some thirty acres. That's the place to hide, thought Russ. He swept the field of his telescope over the large black rocks. For an instant he thought he saw the rear end of a horse, then there was nothing.

Russ shoved his glass into a saddlebag and angled

southwest, again heading for the shallow water he hoped could be found in the bottom of Growler Wash.

Sun Wolf, the Apache, held the horse he had dragged into hiding behind the rock. He watched the pursuers, at the extreme limit of his vision, abandon the trail he and his warriors had made.

Those that followed him rode in a very straight line, maintaining the single file like white horse soldiers. Maybe the alignment was too perfect. As he observed the distant objects, he thought, Was there only one horse being ridden? When it grew dark he would ride down and find the camp and know the answer to the riddle.

Sun Wolf wished he had not been discovered. He wanted to take some of the white men's cattle, not to fight. His band was small, the members much too valuable to lose even one in a battle. And here, in this land, all men were his enemies.

Sun Wolf and his people had slipped north from where they had been hiding in Mexico. Knowing the soldiers still continued the search in the Apache homeland for those Indians refusing to go onto the reservation, he had led his few warriors and their families far to the west. They had come unbidden into the territory of the Cocopah and the Quechan Indians. But these tribes did not need their land, for they had given up their freedom and lived on the small areas of land the white soldiers called reservations.

The Indian returned to the vantage point he had left to hide the horse and again cast his eyes out over the broad desert valley with its scant cover of brush and cactus. Nothing moved, not even a hawk or a buzzard braved the heat to take advantage of the updrafts rising from the hot desert floor. He let his mind sail away to the south end of the mountains where the women and children waited in the hidden camp deep in a narrow canyon.

The warriors had been gone for three days. Soon they

must return with a supply of food, for their families had
been left with a few meager handfuls of grain. The women
would be gathering seed from the heads of the rice grass
now ripe. That was a tedious, unproductive task, but one
could live on the miniature kernels of grain, just barely.

Sun Wolf hoped he could take back meat of the white
man's cattle. But the horses he had just seen would do. He
had eaten many horses.

His five braves slept, stretched out in the narrow slivers
of shade at the base of the larger boulders. Rock That Rolls,
his only son, strong and daring, lay farthest from him.

The young man had been born in a terrible storm. The
wind and rain had come upon Sun Wolf and his woman
while they were camped and awaiting the birth of their
child. They had been lying close together, protected by their
shelter of deer hide and brush. Above them a giant chunk of
rock clung to the slope of a hill. The deluge of rain
weakened the dirt foundation of the monster boulder and it
tore loose, rumbling down upon the small dwelling, striking
the side, ripping it away. Greatly frightened, the woman
went into labor and there in the torrential rain gave birth to a
healthy son, Rock That Rolls.

The Old One, the warrior that had once been called
Raven, rested flat on his back only a few feet from Sun
Wolf. He was so ancient that only Sun Wolf could
remember when the broad streaks of gray had not been in
his hair. And only Sun Wolf, recalling the man's great deeds
of the past, now and then called him Raven.

Due to his great caution and his skill at smelling out and
avoiding ambushes, The Old One continued to survive
while all his comrades were long dead. However, he was a
very brave warrior when the battle began.

The many winters had worked their hardship upon The
Old One. Deep furrows were carved into his face and his
body was merely skin and bones—a stick man, like the

children drew. But like a dry pine knot, he endured, riding the weary daytime miles into night and never once complaining.

Sun Wolf was glad of Raven's presence in the band. His warnings and council to the young impetuous braves would be sorely missed when he no longer existed.

He cast a glance at the old warrior to find the man's eyes studying him.

"What do you see in the valley that worries you, Sun Wolf?" asked Raven. Though both he and Sun Wolf could speak the words of the white man, he spoke in the Apache tongue. For what man would put horse manure in his mouth when he could savor the tones of his own language?

"Some men, and I judge white men, have found our trail and followed it for a finger's width of sun. They came to where we turned toward the mountain and then sat and looked directly at our hiding place. They have now gone away."

"How many were there?" queried Raven.

"Perhaps eight or ten horses. They were very far away and I could not tell if all the horses had riders. I think there was only one man. However many, they go to the valley that lies there." Sun Wolf pointed.

"Why would one man with many horses track us for a distance?" mused The Old One.

"Yes, it is strange. He may have a ranch near here and feels he must know for his own safety."

"That is possible and wise on his part. We have much to learn about the land of the Cocopah and the Quechans."

"It is the white man's land now," Sun Wolf corrected, "and there are very many of them."

"And very few of us," said Raven sorrowfully. "We must be very careful."

"We are enough to take this white man's horses," said

Sun Wolf. He lifted up the Army musket and caressed the heavy steel barrel with his hands.

Russ often glanced at the main peak of the Growler Mountains some four miles distant to the east, trying to remember how it had lain the time before when he had followed the horse trail to water. In the months since he had been there, he was sure several floods had swept the wash. Each one would have reshaped the channel and filled the holes pawed out by the wild mustangs in search of life-sustaining water.

A jackrabbit sprang from the shade at the bottom of a cholla cactus and hurtled along the top of the bank like a gray streak. Russ ignored the rabbit; it meant nothing since the animal could endure for months without water, surviving on the scant moisture in the plants it ate.

The body of the dead horse meant much more. It rested, with its dry skin torn and its ribs bleached white, on the horse path that came down the bank into the bottom of the wash. The carcass indicated high odds there was water close in the gulch.

Half a hundred paces downstream Russ spotted three holes where horses had dug at the sand and gravel. The largest was a yard in diameter and at least two feet deep. A gallon of water filled a small pocket in the bottom of the cavity.

The desert-wise mustangs' keen sense of smell had found water where some impervious obstruction forced it to rise almost to the surface. A man could have died of thirst never knowing water flowed less than an arm's length away.

Russ evaluated the path of the horses. All sign indicated only a small number of animals used the water hole. Even those mustangs traveling many miles to water tarried barely long enough to dig out a drink. They would find little grass on the desert.

Feed grew on the mountain where precipitation fell in greater abundance, and especially on the northern slopes where snow accumulated in the winter and the shade lingered for longer periods of the summer day. Russ had seen these areas of more hospitable climate and knew grass could be found there in moderate quantities.

He removed the shovel from his pack and, starting at the largest hole, began to dig vigorously. An hour later he was pouring sweat. He sagged down to rest. As he sat cooling off, water began to seep into the excavation. Steadily the cool, clear liquid covered the bottom of the cavity.

Russ lay down and drank deeply. After filling his canteen, he untied the horses and allowed them to quench their thirst. Then they were immediately retied as before. He planned always to be ready to ride out fast in case of attack.

Again he labored on the water hole. Periodically he would stop and climb out of the wash and survey his surroundings, searching for enemies in all directions. Finally the excavation had been sunk waist deep and two horse lengths in diameter. The sides were sloped outward at a low angle so the hooves of the cattle would not trample the sand down and cut off the flow too quickly. When he stopped work, there was already a foot of water in the bottom.

Russ changed the saddle from the gray to the less weary roan. Then he pulled off his boots, unbuckled his gun belt, laid it atop the boots, and waded into the deepest part of the water. For five minutes he luxuriated in a bath in the wonderful coolness of the newly created pool. Then he washed his stinking clothing hastily, and donned the sopping garments. He must hurry, it was not safe to be so off guard.

Leaving all the horses in the bottom of the wash, he climbed the bank and, crouching down low, made his way a

short distance to the top of a slight rise of ground covered
with a dense stand of creosote bush.

Silently seating himself, he peered out over the crowns of
the brush. The valley was deserted, all life hiding from the
sizzling sun. Time passed; his clothing dried and he began
to sweat. He could not leave yet and go to the shade at the
base of the mountain, for he wanted any enemy that might
be watching to think he planned to spend the night near the
water.

The sun sank and shadows engulfed the valley. Yet Russ
continued to wait patiently for the light, still diffusing down
from the sky, to die, and for full dusk to arrive. Then, with
visibility only a few hundred yards, he hastened to his
horses, sprang astride, and left at a fast gallop in the
direction of the mountains. There was a lot of distance to
cover and things to do before darkness completely obscured
the land.

He wanted to locate one particular canyon cutting into the
face of the mountain. As best as he could remember, it was
nearly half a mile deep, two hundred yards wide, and with
nearly vertical walls except where it emptied out onto the
floor of the main valley.

Russ found the narrow cleft between tall rock walls.
Anxious to get quickly hidden, he hurried his mounts into
the opening and continued to the extreme upper end.

The horses were hobbled by tying their front legs together
with short lengths of leather strap. The moment Russ freed
them from each other, the horses began to cast around for
something to eat. Their hobbled feet made soft thuds on the
hard ground as they awkwardly hopped about.

Confident the mounts would not work their way out of the
canyon before daylight, Russ rode off on his roan. He found
a location away from the horses near the north wall of the
canyon. Tiredly he climbed down and stood, half leaning,
against his mount in the darkness.

Russ felt nervous and edgy and wanted to be able to leave on a second's notice, so he did not unsaddle. To provide the horse some relief, he released the saddle cinch a notch.

He loosely tied the reins around his wrist. Not bothering to unroll his blankets, he lay down on the sandy ground. The roan nuzzled the man's face, inspecting the strange position of his master. Russ reached out and rubbed the velvety smooth muzzle, glad for the horse's presence, knowing the steadfast, reliable nature of the brute.

Sorry I can't let you loose to graze, old horse, thought Russ. Stay alert and wake me if an enemy comes.

He scraped his hips and shoulders back and forth to shape the soft ground and better cushion his body. He relaxed his tired body. His breathing slowed and steadied. Tuned to the movements of the tall horse standing watch over him, he slept.

Russ awoke in one swift rush of consciousness. He felt the pressure where the reins were pulled tightly on his wrist, and remained perfectly motionless.

The dark outline of the horse's head staring off down the canyon showed against the starlit sky. Its ears were pricked forward, listening, and it sucked gently at some odor on the warm, slow land.

Russ strained to pick up a sound, but could hear nothing. He was completely dependent upon the sharp, primitive senses of the horse.

Several minutes passed and neither man nor animal moved. Then the roan relaxed and dropped its head to rest. Wolf, lion, Indian, or whatever had alerted the horse, was gone.

Russ measured the location of the stars and judged it to be one hour until dawn. He arose, slipped the bit from the horse's mouth, and tied up the bridle reins so the animal would not trip on them. After sliding his rifle from its scabbard, he softly slapped the horse away to graze. The animal liked his company and would not stray far.

Russ sat leaning against the rock of the canyon wall and holding the rifle across his lap. From nearby came a faint noise, a low tearing sound as the horse cropped the stunted desert grass. Russ reached out with his ears, beyond the noise of the mustang, through the distant darkness, listening for every sound.

The remainder of the night slowly spent itself as Russ brooded, thinking about his parents and home, about the violent man Caloon who had accepted him as a partner, but most of all he thought about himself. Could a man who had killed two lawmen, even by mistake, ever return to the companionship of honest men?

Maybe come daylight he would collect the horses and ride straight west to California.

Samantha Tamblin followed her two menfolk to the door of the cabin and stood in the opening until they rode away. Within a hundred yards the deep purple shadows of the early dawn swallowed them. Immediately after the rattle of the iron-shod hooves of the horses had died against the mountainside, she led up her bay mare and saddled her with practiced hands. A short-handled shovel, its blade quickly wrapped in a piece of old tarpaulin, was tied behind the saddle. From under the blanket of her bunk, she extracted a .32-caliber six-gun and strapped it to her waist. A woman's gun, her father had said when he gave it to her.

She stepped to the coal oil lamp and blew down the glass globe to extinguish the flame. Without delay, she picked up a full canteen and swung astride the mare.

She spurred the gray into a rocking-chair lope up the valley. The animal seemed in good spirits and strongly mounted the rough ground that sloped up to the pass that cut through the topmost ridge of the Growlers.

Samantha paid the animal little attention, letting it pick its own way toward the summit while she let her mind drift back over the months that had passed since she and her kin had arrived on the mountain. The winter had hung on cold and windy, not breaking for many days. But the spring finally came, warm and sunny, just in time for the birth of the calves.

These frisky newcomers were growing rapidly and adding their appetite for grass to that of their mothers. That part of the Growlers within a three-mile radius of the cabin could not long sustain this increased demand and would soon be overstocked. More grass and water had to be found.

The evening just past, her father and grandfather had discussed the most favorable direction to expand. Unused land existed in all directions except to the east, where Blackaby's ranch lay. The Tamblins decided the west side of the mountain with its long broad slopes would offer the best new range for their cattle.

Water was the limiting factor to opening up that land. A spring had to be found or perhaps there was water in Growler Wash. The wash would be the easiest to explore so it would be examined first. But the men were worried for they knew the farther they moved to the west, the deeper into rustler territory they would be intruding.

Sam volunteered to make the search while the men finished filling in the gaps of rimrock to fence a summer pasture. They had, with some heat, forbidden her to leave the vicinity of the cabin on such a venture. She explained that Growler Wash was less than ten miles away and easily found. There was no way that she could get lost. Her argument did not sway them at all, but she had silently made her secret plans.

Samantha reached out and stroked the powerful neck of the bay. It stretched its legs a little more at the attention, increasing its speed. Sam laughed at the animal's response. Yes, she thought, today I will find a big water hole and increase the size of our ranch by many thousands of acres.

Chapter 11

Halfway to the top of the Growler Mountains, Samantha halted to give the horse an opportunity to catch its wind. As the animal pulled deep breaths, she looked east at the silent explosion of red and gold fanning out across the eastern sky as the dawn increased. Then, she dropped her view down into the valley to see, for the first time from the mountain, her new home.

The twenty acres of irrigated meadow they had so laboriously leveled could easily be picked out of the desert brush, but the two-room cabin, its dark form squatting beside the spring, was barely visible. No cows were in sight. They had been pushed to the high range so the grass on the lower slopes could be saved for winter feed.

East of the cabin, the valley floor broadened rapidly, growing to nearly two miles wide where it opened out onto the valley of the Ajo. The mountainsides adjacent to the valley reclined at a moderate angle, a slope a cow could climb without much effort to graze the grass and brush.

She was pleased with her family's accomplishments since their arrival on the mountain. But these past months had been filled with work from daylight to dark for all the Tamblins. Her grandfather had laughingly stated that was the way all worthwhile things were gotten.

She glanced at the thick beds of lava rock rimming the valley on the far south side. Somewhere there, her father and grandfather were building a fence. She could see nothing of the men or their horses because of the long distance.

Sam pulled the mare to face the mountain and sent her climbing upward, following the trails the wild animals had selected over thousands of years as the easiest route to get to the pass connecting Ajo Valley with Growler Valley. Off to the right a few hundred yards, a doe and fawn slowly picked their way up toward their daytime bed in the juniper thickets on the higher ridges.

The doe stopped. The fawn nuzzled in close to its mother for comfort. They both watched Sam with sharp eyes until she was out of sight.

Juniper clothed the saddle between the peaks of the mountain and extended onto the drier west face where the trees became stunted and less dense. Sam held to the cover of the trees as she crossed the pass and continued for a little way to the north, until she could look down and see the full length of Growler Valley. She dismounted and dropped the reins, ground tying the mare.

On a soft bed of needles beneath a juniper, she found a seat and leaned back against the bole of the tree. She removed her hat to allow the gentle wind to cool her warm brow, and breathed deeply of the pungent scent of the juniper.

A raucous cawing began, grew louder, and half a score of crows, their thick black wings scooping air, pressing it down to stay aloft, sailed by overhead. They disappeared south along the mountain, still arguing among themselves.

Samantha remembered her father's description of important landmarks located on this side of the mountain and began to pick them out. Straight west, ten miles or so, and half the size of the Growlers, lay the Granite Mountains. Northwest thirty miles, the Palomas Mountains were faintly visible on the hazy horizon. She knew the Gila River passed close to the mountain's southern end.

South of her, twenty miles, the Agua Dulce Mountains could be seen. And five miles beyond that, lay the border between Mexico and the United States.

She started to shift her attention to Growler Valley when, as if by magic, a tiny hummingbird materialized in front of her. Not much more than two yards away, the half-ounce body hung swaying almost imperceptibly in the sunlight. Its brilliant red-orange throat patch and the iridescent brown of its back and sides rivaled the rainbow.

The wings were a blur of movement, emitting a soft buzzing whisper of soft feathers stroking the air at sixty beats per second. As the bird hovered, its needle-billed head, designed to reach deeply into cactus flowers, flicked from side to side as first one bulbous black eye and then the other appraised his strange find.

The hummer glided sideways to a downwind position to catch her scent. Sam's eyes followed the small aerial acrobat as he drifted, stopped, remained suspended as if by some invisible thread, and examined her.

Then, impossibly fast, quicker than she could blink, the bird darted in, closing two thirds of the space between them, stopping a mere arm's length away. Frightened, afraid the hummingbird would mistake her blue eyes for a flower and plunge that long bill into them, Sam clamped her eyelids tightly closed and held them that way for a few excited heartbeats.

Cautiously, she opened her eyes a crack and saw nothing; she widened her eyes more, and looked quickly around. The hummingbird had vanished as swiftly and silently as it had arrived.

She felt a little foolish, sorry it was gone. And for just a moment, she felt a little lonely on the top of the tall mountain.

She raised up to see if the mare had gotten her wind back and was ready to make the descent into the valley. The animal stood tense, attention fastened on something in the juniper.

Sam never heard the approaching horse, until suddenly a young man on a tall roan rode into the clearing. She started hastily to rise. His horse saw her and stopped stone still.

The man's hand flashed down and up and the black deadly eye of a six-gun pointed unerringly at her. The weapon threatened her for an instant, then disappeared into its holster.

Apprehension showed on the man's face and Sam wondered how close she had come to getting shot. His expression changed and gimlet eyes touched her horse, swept the patch of trees all around and the hillside beyond.

Now the stranger's attention settled on her, regarding her with a stern yet quizzical countenance. Sam straightened her body and steadily returned his look.

He was tall, and clothed in rumpled, dusty clothing. A youthful blond beard, not many days old, covered a face burned brown.

His left hand moved, sweeping the battered hat from his head. The skin above the demarcation line where his hat had protected him from the sun was startlingly white.

"Hello," said Russ. "You don't act like you're lost, but do you need any help?"

"No, I'm not lost," responded Sam and volunteered no further information. There was a tone in his voice, disapproval maybe, that she did not like. He had no right to make a judgment about her. He was not all that much older than she was.

Russ was still partially stunned by the unexpected appearance of the girl. Primed for an attack by the Indians, he had come frighteningly close to triggering his gun at her when she had risen from under the tree. What was keeping him even more off balance was the striking beauty of her.

He wasn't quite sure that she wasn't a lovely spirit teasing him with wide innocent eyes. However, spirits did not wear pistols strapped to their sides, although she seemed to have forgotten hers was there.

"What in the hell are you doing on top of Growler Mountain?" he asked in a voice that was slightly hoarse.

"And why shouldn't I be on Growler? I have as much right here as you or anybody else." She doubted that was really true. When he had come upon her, his reflex action had been to draw his gun in readiness to fight, or to kill if the need was there. While she had been greatly surprised at the sudden meeting, no thought of defense or attack had entered her mind.

"Maybe so, but there are six Indian warriors about three miles north of here that might not see it that way. At least they were in that location late yesterday. If they had come onto you instead of me, this parley might be going a lot worse for you. Where did you come from and which way are you going?"

She did not like his attitude, his direct questioning as if she were a child, or someone not quite right in the head. But the mentioning of the Indians so near sent a chill through her. She examined the man's face to see if it was a joke or some trick.

Russ felt the girl's eyes, unnaturally large and piercing, probing his thoughts. Felt them as if she were touching him, caressing him. And the thought of a caress from her caused his pulse to race. This was why the outlaws had broken their

rule of only making one cattle drive to Mexico each year; it
was to find a female such as this one. No, not such as this
one. Russ was certain he had before him a very rare
specimen. One in many thousands of young women.

But what should he do? What could he do in the short
time before Raasleer arrived? The Indians must not capture
her. Surely Raasleer's gang could not be allowed to find her.
And yet, there she stood, slightly scrappy, and acting as if
no danger existed.

Samantha smiled to herself at the change of expression on
his face. He wore a serious, worried frown.

"We have a ranch over there"—she turned to point—"at
the base of the mountain where there is a big spring."

"I know the place. Camped there a year or so ago. You
folks must have moved in recently."

Sam nodded. "Snow was still on the ground." She
recalled the two cold months they had lived in the open until
the men had hauled in the logs, and collected the rocks to
build the cabin.

"Where are you heading now?"

"Down to the bottom of the valley to see if I can find any
water in the creek bed."

Russ shook his head in the negative. "Appears best to me
that you should hightail it back to your ranch and tell your
menfolk about the Indians. You wouldn't want them to get
scalped." He looked sharply at her in warning. "They
would also take a pretty white girl if they happened on to
her."

Should she trust what the man said? Was there some other
reason he did not want her to go into Growler Valley? She
cast a glance past him, down into the desert basin.

Russ saw and understood her suspicion. He was a
complete stranger to her and she had no reason to believe
him.

"There is one thing that I can tell you that might be

helpful. Straight west of here, in the wash, there's considerable water. It's not on the surface, you have to dig about two feet or so down in the gravel. I dug out a hole yesterday evening and found plenty of water to supply a hundred cows or more in a permanent way. After each flood it would have to be opened up again. Lot of loose sand and gravel in the bottom that moves with the run-off and will fill any hole right back up."

Russ replaced his hat. "Come. I'll point out the place to you where I found the water. I think we can see it well enough from up here that you can find it easy when you do go down to search."

Without a word, Sam strode to her horse and, lifting her foot up to the stirrup, hoisted herself into the saddle. Russ watched her young woman's body move beneath the heavy cloth of her riding pants. Beautiful, he thought. Beautiful.

They rode a few hundred feet down the slope to the edge of the juniper. Sam halted the mare and sensed the man had stopped very near her. He said nothing, staring searchingly toward the north end of the valley. For a long moment he was absorbed in his scrutiny. Then, seemingly satisfied at what he had seen, or not seen, he looked down into the basin in front of them and pointed.

"Do you see that big bend in the channel, the largest one and due west of us?" he asked.

"You mean the one that curves away from us?"

"Yes, that's it. Well, downstream about three hundred yards is where I located the water. Good water and plenty of it. I had some and it had no bad effect on me at all."

"How do you know there is a lot of water?"

Sam saw the hint of irritation on his face and wondered why the question bothered him.

"I dug a hole large enough to take a bath in," he said shortly. At least that was half true, he thought. "Will you please"—and he stressed the last word—"go home for now? It's not safe for you and I must be traveling on."

"Well, if it's so dangerous, why are you here?"

Russ put his hand on the stock of the rifle that hung beneath his left leg. He was not afraid at all for his own safety. He was cautious, yes, and ready for action, but there was no fear of the danger that surely lay ahead. He laughed at the revelation.

Sam saw the large calloused hand fondle the weapon, heard the laugh. More strongly than ever before in her life, she sensed the immense feeling of independence, the freedom from fear that a strong man could possess. She could never have the strength of a man, however she could acquire equal skill with weapons. Beginning immediately she would practice in earnest with rifle and pistol.

"I'll ride back to the other side of the pass with you, if that's all right," said Russ.

Without speaking, Sam and Russ crossed through the pass. At the first down slope, she pulled rein and turned to look directly into the lean, hard face.

"Our house is down where the bottom flattens out and on the left side of the stream."

"Yes, I know where the spring is," said Russ.

Their eyes held and silence settled upon them. A breeze reached them and made pleasant sounds in the juniper. For Russ it was a very enjoyable span of time.

Was it possible she was reluctant to leave because of him? Perhaps he could ride with her partway to her home. Then the thought of the Englishman and his crew of cowboys riding hard to catch Raasleer and regain the stolen cattle pushed that idea from his mind. He had to get to the lookout. Caloon was his friend and had to be protected.

"I had better go," said Sam and averted her face. "Good-bye."

Russ felt a sad loss when the perfect oval of her face and

the intelligent blue eyes could no longer be seen. He probably would never see her again. "Good-bye."

Sam set a fast pace down the rocky trail. Her father and grandfather had to be warned about the Indians. If they were as close as the man had said, there was no time to waste.

She suddenly yanked the mare back on her haunches and looked up the mountainside. Why hadn't she asked the man's name? Jerking off her hat, she waved it vigorously back and forth above her head in a large arc.

Almost instantly she saw movement in the edge of the juniper and could make out the man waving his hat in return. Then he vanished into the trees.

Chapter 12

Russ rode hurriedly, yet cautiously, climbing steeply around the west side of the mountain. The morning was far advanced and he was unsure how close Raasleer might be. Or the Englishman, who would surely be trailing the rustlers or riding fast to head them off from reaching the safety of Mexico.

Half an hour later, Russ was seated on the highest, most western extremity of the towering bulk of the mountain. He aimed the telescope out across the sun-drenched desert and methodically began to glass the terrain.

Close in the sparse cactus and brush gave the flat land of the valley a faint pastel-green tinge. The color changed to a dark brown as the field of the spyglass ranged miles to the north. One odd-shaped patch of brown, too far away to determine its exact nature, stirred his interest. He carefully marked its location for later checking.

He turned the glass down along the side of the mountain, trying to spot the horses he had left in a grassy cove just below the pass. They were there, contentedly grazing.

Russ again swiveled his spyglass to the north and after a

time the brown patch took form, becoming a tall, wavering column of dust sailing two or three hundred feet up on the heated air. At the base of the dust cloud, the forms of cows like small red ants steadily approached.

Russ was surprised and dismayed at the quantity of the dust. That aerial mark could be seen for miles by the Englishman, or the Indians. Russ judged the only question was which one of them would locate the herd first.

The Englishman would be coming from the north. Where was he? Try as he might, Russ could see no sign of pursuit.

At some time short of noon, with the stolen herd large in the telescope, Russ made one last effort to spot the rightful owner of the cattle or any other moving thing. He detected no sign of danger. The Indians, however, could be waiting in ambush in any one of innumerable hidden places. He left the lookout and traveled down from the mountain, collecting the horses from the glade as he went.

He reached the water hole first and waited for the herd and riders to arrive. They were soon visible, picking their way through the brush, their shapes wavering and indistinct in pale streamers of dust.

Caloon rode three or four hundred yards out in front on point, as he had said he would. His plan was laid. If Russ was not there, he would spur like hell to get away from Raasleer and the remainder of the gang. Then he saw Russ sitting his horse on a small rise near the dry watercourse.

Russ watched Caloon draw close, saw the dust lying heavy on man and horse. Caloon looked at him with tired eyes, red holes in his sun-browned face.

"You damn fool," Caloon said curtly, "why are you still here?" Without waiting for an answer, he continued on past and down to the water.

Russ was astonished at Caloon's uncompanionable greeting and the words rankled him. What he did was his own business. He followed Caloon into the wash, but stayed some distance behind, watching the man kneel and bathe his face in the fresh water.

Raasleer and the remainder of the rustler gang, abandoning the cows which had not yet smelled the water, spurred in swiftly. They climbed down from their mounts and gathered stiff and weary in a group on the lip of the water hole. Then with a wild whoop, they unbuckled their holstered six-guns, let them fall, and charged into the clean, clear water.

Finally, Raasleer rose to his feet and looked at Russ. "Have you seen anything? Is the Englishman after us yet?"

"Nothing in sight as late as an hour ago when I left the mountain," answered Russ.

"In an hour a man on horseback can travel a long ways and so could be very close. Anything else I should know?"

"I saw the tracks of six Indian ponies yesterday afternoon on the north end of the Growler. I crossed the same tracks again about two miles back. They were heading to the south. I would guess the braves are looking for trouble. The dust from the heifers may draw them."

"The Englishman behind, and Indians ahead. That doesn't sound very good. Corddry told me he heard there was a new ranch on the Growlers. Have you seen any cows or riders?"

Raasleer's knowledge of the existence of the ranch surprised Russ and he hesitated in answering. The girl had to be protected, so he chose his words carefully.

"Nope. I saw neither cows nor men. I wouldn't think the Growlers would be a good place to start a ranch."

"Maybe not, but there's always fools around that will try anything. No one is going to set up a spread any place close to the route I use to get to Mexico. That would mean they could see my comings and goings and be dangerous to me. We'll look the other side of the mountain over carefully on our way back. Anyone there is going to get a hard time."

Russ wondered if they were fools or very brave people. He thought the latter was more accurate.

Raasleer picked up his hat and put it on his wet head. "For now, the men and animals must have rest. You go partway back up the side of the mountain and keep watch for another four hours or so. Then come down and help us drive south. If you see anything wrong you come whipping and spurring to warn us."

Russ led his roan to the eight fresh horses tied on the bank above the wash. He needed a change of mounts and since the gray gelding had proven itself a strong, reliable animal, the saddle was quickly swapped to its broad back.

The heifers had finally sensed the water and came trotting tiredly past Russ as he left the wash. Good quality breeding stock, he thought. The Englishman will certainly be coming with many armed men to take them back.

Russ worked upward toward a high vantage point. Often he looked at the divide between the two main peaks of the mountain where the girl had been. She and her family were in great peril and he did not know what to do about it, how he could help them, or if he should.

For days, ever since the killing of the two marshals, Russ had been wandering aimlessly. Now with a surge of excitement, he knew what he could do to make his life have some meaning, a purpose. He would become the protector of the girl of the mountain.

Russ knew the danger was very real. Soon, the livestock of the girl's family would be grazing in Growler Valley, easily found by the rustler gang. What would Raasleer do when he discovered them? Russ knew the answer. The rustler would steal the cattle and whoever tried to stop him would be killed. Unless Russ stopped him.

She would never know, but he would always be in the place most likely to give him a chance to help her, and the gun that had killed by mistake would kill again if needed.

He felt lighthearted with his decision. For the first time in many days, he felt somewhat good about himself.

Raasleer was awake and on guard when Russ returned to the herd of cattle. All the other men had changed their riding gear to rested horses and now slept on the hard ground in the scant shade cast by the brush and cactus. The cattle lay scattered about resting.

"Nothing in sight," said Russ to Raasleer's unasked question. "The Englishman must not have checked on his livestock today."

Raasleer nodded. "Or maybe he looked at them late in the day and is on his way. He'll inspect them tomorrow for sure." He glanced up, marking the height of the sun. "It will be dark in five hours or so. If we can stay clear of trouble and not get hit for that long, we'll have the whole night to travel and be in Mexico before dawn."

"How much of a drive do we have to make once we're across the border?"

"Takes two days or so to a Mex town I know where they will buy these critters without one question being asked about where they came from. Are you looking forward to the pretty, dark-eyed *señoritas?*"

Russ grinned to hide his thoughts and pictured in his mind the beautiful face of the girl on the mountain. That was who he would like to see again. But she would want nothing to do with a killer and thief. He could not blame her.

Raasleer's voice broke in on Russ. "Get all the heifers rounded up and heading south while I wake the men."

As Russ rode into the brush, he heard Raasleer calling loudly to the men. "On your feet. You can sleep in two more days. And you'll have company in your beds." He laughed coarsely.

The exhausted heifers did not want to move and Russ practically had to ride his horse right on top of them before they climbed reluctantly to their feet. He had not located all of them in the high brush before Caloon and most of the other men came to assist in the search.

Two men rapidly began to fill in the hole Russ had so laboriously dug. When they finished, several horses were led back and forth across the location until all sign of the excavation was erased.

Soon, the herd was moving, plodding at a slow man's walk. The hundreds of hooves spun a new pall of dust that rose up to be sharply outlined against the pale blue sky.

The white puffy clouds that had begun to form shortly after midday continued to grow and move to the north. Russ, noting the darkening shadows, looked up to measure the towering masses of moisture. The larger ones were thick, boiling up with great vigor.

Immediately south, a score of miles, an especially large cloud was dark gray and shaped like a mammoth anvil. Its flatly beveled base stretched for a space greater than the width of the Growler Mountains. Above the thick base, the trunk of the cloud climbed vertically for more than four miles, daringly reaching into the cold upper sky where only ice crystals could exist. Its extreme top was deformed, blown outward to the north in a sharp, overhanging lip, by winds more violent than the surface of the earth had ever experienced.

Raasleer, observing the direction of Russ's view, spoke. "We'll have thunderstorms before the evening is over."

"Yes," agreed Russ. "And there could be hail, too."

Lightning, like the flash of a rifle at night, bridged the gap between the cloud and the ground. Thunder rumbled menacingly.

As the storm cloud closed in on the riders and cows, the wind picked up strength, catching the dust and rolling it forward like the fog off a winter sea. Russ could not see Raasleer or the heifers in the gritty brown maelstrom.

A shot rang out, then a flurry of them crashed. Loud voices, screaming maniacally, sliced through the wind. The dust, suddenly split by some sudden quirk of the air current, exposed the herd and half a dozen Indians on horseback charging through the mass of animals from the right.

The front part of the frightened herd stampeded straight ahead down the valley toward Mexico. A few animals raced ahead of the Indians in the direction of the Growlers. Fifty or so spooked back the way they had so wearily trod.

Before Russ could touch his gray horse with spurs and try to stop the runaway heifers, one Indian brave, just a boy, raced past, thirty or forty yards in front of Raasleer and himself.

The outlaw leader drew and fired in one fluid movement. The Indian jerked at the strike of the bullet and fell sideways from his running mustang. He caught himself just when there seemed no chance for recovery and pulled himself back up into the saddle. The warrior threw himself forward and clasped the powerful neck of the horse with both arms. The horse plunged into the dust and disappeared.

"Goddamn it. Only winged him," cursed Raasleer as the brown dust swirled in to reduce their vision to a few feet.

Russ marveled at the skill of the outlaw, drawing his six-gun and hitting a man on a running horse at that long range. And yet Raasleer was angry that he had only wounded the Indian.

Raasleer shouted at Russ over the noise of the wind and pointed to the east. "You go fetch back those that went toward the mountain. And hurry it up, for this delay will give the Englishman a chance to catch up with us."

As Russ urged the gray in pursuit, lightning flashed from the nearby thunderhead and rain began to spill just a short distance down the valley. The big horse, excited by the stampede, the gunshots, and the approaching storm, bolted across the plain. Like an agile antelope, he dodged the tall saguaro and ocotillo cactus and jumped the low-growing creosote brush and pear cactus.

Russ concentrated his eyes in front, swept them over the brush, rock, and ground, anticipating what the horse might do next, and let the animal run. He was exhilarated by the race, by the feel of the broad muscular back moving between his legs and the sharp wind on his face. In the pure joy of the moment, he yelled at the top of his lungs and continued until his throat burned. He slapped the neck of the mustang. "Run you big bastard, run! Yahoo!" And he laughed.

The horse finally slowed of its own volition and Russ began to scan the land. He had thought the tired heifers would soon run themselves out, but he did not catch up with any of them until he was close to a shoulder of the mountain that shoved out into the valley. When he came to the cattle, they stood with drooping, dry muzzles nearly touching the ground and sides heaving spasmodically.

He began to circle through the brush, rounding up the cattle. It was a difficult task to find them, however; in twenty minutes, he had collected thirty.

He left the bunched cattle and headed in a straight line for the foot of the mountain less than a quarter mile away. From that higher land, he could look down into the brush and perhaps locate animals he had missed.

He moved swiftly and soon was above the valley floor. The wind was much stronger. He surveyed the land spread below and spotted one heifer that had been overlooked.

A lightning bolt lashed down to smite the side of the mountain and thunder crashed. Some animal, startled by the ear-splitting noise, stirred in the brush, an easy rifle shot away. Russ caught the motion from the corner of his eye and pivoted to look.

He saw nothing now, but was positive there had been something there. Pulling his carbine and holding it ready across the saddle in front of him, he eased the gray through the brush and rock.

Then Russ saw what had moved at the lightning strike. A horse lay in one of the larger patches of brush. It was an Indian pony carrying a cheap Mexican saddle and a leather halter. As Russ drew close, the pony scrambled to its feet and, as if awaiting instructions, looked down at a man sprawled on the ground.

There were no visible wounds on the mustang. The well-trained horse had lain in the brush at the orders of its master, so they would not be seen by an enemy.

Its owner was the young warrior Raasleer had shot. He lay in the dirt, unconscious and not knowing he had been found. A nasty wound gaped open on the top of his left arm. Blood leaked steadily, puddling in a large semi-congealed mass on the ground. He had already lost much of the precious fluid.

Russ stepped down hastily, leaned over the fallen man, and clamped the bullet-mangled flesh with his hand. He squeezed until the red flow stopped.

Wind whipped the brush wildly. Lightning flashed, searing bright, and thunder roared. Cool dampness rode the wind. It would be raining in a moment. What was he to do with the seriously injured Indian? If he left, the man would surely die.

Russ began to pull his neckerchief free to make a tourniquet. At that instant, the end of a rifle barrel slammed into the side of his face. He rocked back under the hard blow, threw his eyes to the side to see the danger, and his bloody right hand plunged for his six-gun.

He stopped his draw. He was too late. A large-bored musket was aimed point-blank at his heart by a tall Indian. At the close range, there would be no chance the Indian would miss.

The black eyes in the hating face meant death for Russ. A brown finger tightened on the trigger.

Another Indian, a small old man, was suddenly there. He grabbed the first man's arm and shoved it up until the musket no longer pointed at the white man. In a tongue Russ could not comprehend, the old Indian spoke rapidly to the larger man.

They stood locked rigidly together. The white hair of the old man, caught by the wind from behind, stood erect like the mane of some ancient lion. The muscular arm that could crush the old man with one blow made no effort to force the gun back down, but the menacing eyes of the man with the musket never left Russ's face.

Raven released his hold on Sun Wolf and turned to Russ. "Stop the bleeding. Tie it tightly here." He touched a spot above the wound on Rock That Rolls's arm.

Russ jerked his neckerchief loose and cinched it firmly around the arm until the blood was forced to stop. Raven hurried to his horse, standing nearby, and dug a small deer-hide pouch from a saddlebag. He returned quickly, knelt beside Rock That Rolls, and spread the contents of the pouch on his slow-breathing chest.

Raven handed a sharp iron needle and length of thread to Russ. "Thread this. My eyes are old and cannot see well."

Russ wiped his bloody hand, and took the thread and needle. Raven opened a small metal tin in preparation for using the brown salve it contained.

As Raven accepted the needle from Russ, he said, "It is best to help a man while he still is not able to feel the pain. That way he will not cry out and dishonor himself."

Raven pressed the raw edges of flesh tightly together, and using all the skill gleaned by tending a hundred such injuries, sewed the red lips of the wound expertly closed. He liberally covered his handiwork with salve.

Raven spoke to Sun Wolf in their native tongue. "That will hold if we move him carefully."

"What should we do with the *gringo?*" asked Sun Wolf, using the Mexican name for an American.

"He was helping your son to stay alive. Don't you owe him much?"

"It would be better to have one less enemy. One more white-eye dead."

"What does one more enemy mean when we have thousands of them? And this one perhaps could be a friend."

"I do not believe that could happen. But you have rightly asked for his life to be spared."

Sun Wolf jabbed a finger at Russ's horse. "Go. But thank Raven for your life. For I would surely kill you. Go now!"

Russ moved to his mount. As he hoisted himself astride, large cold drops of rain began to fall, striking the men, the horses, and drumming on the hard ground. He smelled the rain, tasted the fresh liquid on his lips.

He started to rein his horse away, then hesitated and turned back to look at the gaunt Indians. The eyes of the old man called Raven glowed with savage pride. Russ knew the old Indian's pride and belief in what was fair had saved his life.

Russ held up his hand and extended all five fingers. Above the tumult of the storm he shouted, "Down there," and he pointed at the heifers bunched in the rain. "I will leave you five cows. May you and your women and children live well this winter."

He spurred away from the Indians, down the rocky slope. From his blanket roll he pulled his rain slicker and tugged it on over his wet clothing.

He glanced back once, and saw the chilling rain had wiped out the mountain. Had swallowed the Indians.

Chapter 13

Russ rode drag, bringing up the rear of the herd, following the heifers as they ghosted across the night-shadowed plain.

It was near midnight. The sky was cloudless, the fast-moving storm having already worked its way beyond the northern horizon. Now a great silver cannonball of a moon climbed its trajectory through the heavens.

Russ had joined the main drive with his catch of stampeded cattle just at dark and in a driving rain. Raasleer had taken advantage of the pouring rain and had turned the herd directly west. For more than four hours they drove through the storm. Before the rain stopped they had crossed Growler Valley and climbed up and over the backbone of the narrow Granite Mountains.

When the rain finally abated, the rustler leader called his men together. They sat their horses silently in the murk and waited for him to explain the next move.

Raasleer spoke. "That was a timely storm. We're now in a valley about a mile wide that extends clear into Mexico.

That mountain range we crossed will keep us out of sight of the Englishman—if he's coming."

He surveyed the wet and tired riders in the moonlight. "We should be safe now. When it gets close to daylight, we'll send someone up to just this side of the ridge of the mountain. He can watch the valley to the east. That way we won't be surprised. Now let's move these critters fast as we can to Mexico."

Russ measured the heifers. They badly needed rest and a chance to graze. But that would have to wait until much later. One animal stopped and Russ prodded the weary brute back into motion with a snap of the end of his rope on its rump.

Raasleer came riding in from the left, drifting soundlessly through the desert brush and drew near Russ. "Everything all right?" he asked.

Russ looked at the man's face, distorted and animal-like in the moonlight. He did not trust the man. Caloon's suspicions were catching. "I need some help. It's hard to see all the stragglers and I may lose some."

"Yeah, we lost three last night. I'll send someone to give you a hand."

"How many head do we have since the stampede?"

"I counted 183. Still plenty to make a good payday. There'll be somebody back here in a little while to help." Raasleer angled off to the right, continuing his circuit of the herd, and was soon lost to sight.

A quarter hour later a horseman materialized from the gloom and came toward Russ. "Hello," called Caloon.

"Hello, yourself. Do you plan to work drag with me?" asked Russ.

"Yep."

They rode along together. Neither spoke. The herd had long since left the land wet by the storm and the smell of dust hung heavy in the men's nostrils.

"I've eaten enough dust to start a potato patch," said Russ.

Caloon chuckled and Russ joined in. Even as he laughed, Russ reflected that there was damn little to joke about while driving a stolen herd of cattle with the owner maybe just out there in the edge of the darkness ready to come in shooting. The humorous feeling vanished.

Russ let his mind recall the beautiful girl of the Growler Mountains. He pictured her face in his mind, remembering the gentle tones of her voice and eyes clear as crystal. Was she still safe in this perilous land? He rode with Raasleer and thus knew where that danger was. There were the Indians, however. They seemed intent on stealing cattle. What would they do if they happened upon the isolated ranch?

The moon crested the highest point of its flight and began the long fall to the western rim of the world. The night became darker just before dawn. Russ pondered his questions.

"What do you think of driving cattle at night?" Caloon's voice yanked Russ back to the present.

Russ hesitated a moment before answering. "I guess as rustlers we had better get to liking it."

"Russ, you don't have to get used to it. Why didn't you leave when you had a good chance?"

"I've killed two lawmen, and another man who was not my enemy. Now I've stolen a man's cattle. Hell, I'm as bad as any one of Raasleer's gang."

"Yep, you've done all those things. And none of it means as much as a fart in a windstorm."

"What do you mean? How can it be anything but murder and stealing?"

"If you could look into the backtrail of all the men in the Arizona Territory, you would find that just about every one of them had done something against the law. They've either robbed somebody of their hard-earned money, or put their brand on someone else's calf. Several of them have even killed other men. But, you know, the difference between this gang and those men is they up and called it quits and now play it fair and square. You can do the same if you want."

"I would like that," said Russ, thinking of the girl again, "but I don't believe I can ever feel right around honest people again."

"You got a kink in your mind that needs to be straightened out," said Caloon. "You're as good as any-body else. Remember this, the longer you wait to try going it law-abiding, the less chance you'll have in carrying it off."

"What you say makes some sense. I just can't do it now."

"It's your life."

"Yes it is," said Russ sharply. He was instantly sorry for the tone of his answer for he felt Caloon was his friend. The man's statement had a lot of truth in it.

To get his mind onto another track, Russ spoke to Caloon. "I didn't see Berdugo after the stampede. Where did he go?"

"Raasleer sent him off on a fast ride to the south soon as the storm got over. I never heard what the trip was for. Maybe to line up buyers for the cattle."

"If that's so, I hope he finds somebody who'll pay a fair price."

"Yeah, but what's a fair price for stolen cattle?" asked Caloon. He glanced at a knot of heifers. "I think I see some animals that are acting like they want to stop and lay down. I'm going to mosey over there and change their minds." He reined away.

The sun was a sullen red orb, hanging low in the evening sky as the Englishman, Jeffery Edmonton, led the way, riding hard. His band of twelve heavily armed cowboys followed after him along the tracks of the herd of heifers.

One of Edmonton's riders had discovered the high-grade cattle missing from the meadow on the Gila River in mid-afternoon. In less than an hour and leading a loaded packhorse, the men had struck the trail. The pursuit was swift, yet the tracks, growing indistinct in the weakening light, stretched empty before them.

Edmonton suddenly pulled his horse to a halt. His crew drew rein beside him. "No more tracks," said Edmonton. "They have all vanished, been washed away."

Ken Shallow, a large muscular man and the ranch foreman, guided his mount up beside his boss. "That storm we saw from a distance had heavy rain in it. We won't find sign again until we get beyond the bounds of it."

"This will slow us down a great deal," said Edmonton. "It's getting dark fast and I doubt we can straighten this trail out before we can't see the sign at all."

"No need to waste time here. The rustlers are surely heading for Mexico, taking the most direct way to get there."

Edmonton looked at Shallow through the deepening darkness. The man was good, had proven it many times during the past several weeks, most recently by correctly interpreting the sign the outlaws had made in the dry wash back a few miles. There he had told the men where to dig for water. In twenty minutes enough of the precious liquid had been found to satisfy the men and horses.

"I understand you're suggesting we strike out due south and hope to see the rustlers at daybreak. But we might angle off from the route they take and be miles from them. Then we wouldn't know whether to go east or west to pick up their trail once again."

Shallow measured the ranch owner. The Englishman was smart and trying hard to be a cattleman. But he was too damned inexperienced. Old John Blackaby would not need to be told how to follow the cows through the night. However, Shallow knew that was why Blackaby had arranged for him to be foreman, to protect his half interest in the new ranch.

"I was thinking of a better idea than that," said Shallow. "Every two or three miles a dry wash drains down from the Growlers. The sides of the cuts are usually steep and the bottoms have little vegetation. Now, two hundred cows tear up the ground quite a bit and the moon will be full tonight and be up in an hour or so. It won't be easy, but once we get beyond where it rained, we'll be able to find sign in those washes. When we strike one, the bulk of the men will stop and rest their horses while a man goes each way along the bank on foot until one finds tracks. He'll call out and we'll all continue south, at the same time angling toward the location of the rustler's route."

"Has a good chance of working," said Edmonton. "It'll take a lot of riding and looking if we're to catch them before they cross into Mexico."

"We'll find their trail even if one of us has to walk the full distance to the Mex border."

Edmonton laughed savagely. "Goddamn, even with the storm, I feel like we're going to have good fortune and capture them. We'll have a hanging party tomorrow."

Shallow liked the toughness in the Englishman's voice, but he was less certain about catching the men with the cattle. If this was Raasleer's gang with the cattle, and he felt strongly it was, then their quarry might slip away as they had done from other posses so many times before.

Further, several horses had come in from the east and joined the herd at the water hole. Were they additional gang members or fresh mounts for the outlaws to use to outrun any pursuit? If nine or ten more rustlers were with the cattle, that would mean a deadly fight. Shallow looked at Edmonton. How would the Englishman's courage hold up when the lead started flying past his ears?

"Ken, you take the lead, straight south toward the border," said Edmonton.

"Yes, sir," said Shallow and moved off into the grayness with Edmonton close beside him.

"Do you think we're gaining on them?" asked Edmonton.

"Yes, I think so," said Shallow. "The cattle must be worn down and traveling slow for they've covered many rough miles. Soon they'll drop down and refuse to move. That's when we'll catch them."

"The rustlers must know we could ride them down if we found the cattle missing soon after they were taken. They could be waiting in ambush for us."

"You're right," agreed Shallow. "If we're following their trail at daylight, that could be a dangerous time. But we're a long ways from getting so close they would feel threatened enough to try to ambush us. Just in case, though, we'll be ready when light comes."

"Do you think it's the rustler called Raasleer?"

"If I was to make a guess, I would say it was. The man has had a lot of success in stealing cattle. Much too much, I say. That makes a man grow bold, and maybe a little careless. With luck we may find out who they are tomorrow."

"I surely want to get those heifers back for myself and Blackaby. Pass the word to the men there'll be a bonus in it for them if we succeed."

In the half darkness, Edmonton saw Shallow shake his head. "That ain't necessary. Chasing rustlers is just part of a cowhand's job. They don't expect any extra pay. If you catch one resting in the shade when the sun is hot enough to melt a rock, look the other way. That's the kind of pay they appreciate."

"That's a border marker," said Corddry, flicking his thumb at a waist-high mound of dark-colored rock. "We are now entering Mexico. For you who haven't been this way before, there's a pile of rock every mile east and west. The Army spent months building them after the Mexicans were kicked south."

Not one of the weary riders within hearing bothered to acknowledge Corddry's comments. As the long miles had passed, the pace of the spent and footsore herd had slackened to a crawl. Now, except for one man on point, all the rustlers rode at the rear. They were constantly busy prodding the animals onward.

Caloon edged his mount beside Russ. "We may be in Mexico, but I don't think that makes any difference. If you were trailing your stolen herd of cattle, would you stop at the border?"

"No," answered Russ, shaking his head. "It wouldn't mean a thing to me."

"Neither will it to the Englishman. By now he must know his heifers are missing. We can barely keep them moving. Soon they will plumb stop. With those savvy cowboys of his, he'll find us."

"You think Raasleer has got us into a bind we can't get out of?" asked Russ, looking into Caloon's tired, drawn face.

"I don't know. He's actin' plenty nervous."

"Which direction do you think they'll hit us from if they catch up?"

Caloon shrugged his shoulders. "Most likely from the front or side. Best way for them would be to get ahead and let us ride into them."

"What in tarnation is going on!" exclaimed Russ. "Here comes the point man riding like all hell is after him."

"The Englishman can't have got ahead of us yet," responded Caloon. "He couldn't do it in the dark and it's just now barely daylight."

The man raced up to Raasleer. "Riders coming, fifteen to twenty. They just came out from behind that point of hill, spotted us, and are coming fast."

Raasleer emitted a stentorian yell to get all his men's attention. "Everybody come with me. Get your guns ready. I don't aim to lose this herd now that we're so close to getting gold coin for them." He spurred and his horse sprang into a full run.

Raasleer pulled up a hundred yards in front of the herd. "Spread out about ten feet apart and stay primed," he commanded. "Pick your targets soon as they stop. If I pull my gun, you all start shooting."

The strange horsemen approached swiftly, the hooves of their mounts beating a loud rumble on the hard ground. In the slanting rays of the early morning sun, bright metallic arrows reflected from their weapons.

Raasleer saw the oversized sombreros with the broad turned-up brims. A moment later he made out the swarthy faces. "Mexican bandits!" he cried to his gang of rustlers.

Russ counted the heavily armed men, most with bandoleers across their shoulders. Some wore two belts of cartridges, making a cross in the center of their chests. "Fifteen of them. Do you think they take us for ranch hands out with a herd?"

Raasleer's glance, hot and fierce, swept past Corddry and Caloon and caught Russ's eye for a second. He grinned, showing all his teeth, then looked back at the bandits.

"What damn bad luck," Corddry said to Raasleer. "I thought we were going to make it without any trouble."

"It's a good thing they did not see us first and hide and

attack us from cover," said Raasleer. "We wouldn't have had much of a chance then." He loosened his pistol in its holster and looked hastily left and right to check the readiness of his men. Though outnumbered more than two to one, they still had a chance to come through this with most of them alive. He had seen all his men in action and knew they were exceptionally good with guns.

Grudgingly he admitted to himself Caloon was very good. The kid, Russ, was even better.

The bandits stopped a hundred yards out and spoke briefly among themselves. Then they came on, walking their steeds and fanning out on both sides of the chief.

"Sons of bitches act like they mean business," said Kanttner from Russ's right.

Russ felt his blood rushing. He flashed a look at Caloon, next to him on the left, saw him watching the Mexicans from squinted eyes, his hand resting ready near his six-gun.

Corddry sat his horse next in line, then Raasleer. The two remaining rustlers, Gredler and Banty, were lined up beyond the leader.

The bandits were equally divided on both sides of their chief. Russ noted that fact and judged one more man should be with the two rustlers on Raasleer's left to even up the strength on that side. Too late now to make that correction.

"There's going to be some killing in a minute," said Caloon in a matter-of-fact voice.

Chapter 14

━━━━━━━━━━━━━━━━━━━━━━━

"There's a hell of a lot of them," said Raasleer, critically gauging the long line of bandits drawing close. "But some of their weapons are old and, I hope, not too good. If the chief starts to give an order to the others to attack us, I'll shoot him. The rest of you open up on the men in front of you. Kill every one of them if the shooting begins."

The tension hung heavy between the two bands of men, making the hair on the nape of Russ's neck twist as if a lightning bolt was about to strike. The dark, bearded faces seemed extremely menacing. His mind chilled with the excitement and danger of the coming battle. He pulled a breath of fresh air deeply into his lungs and let it out slowly.

The bandits stopped not thirty feet distant. The chief was a squat, powerful man on a good black horse.

"Gringos," he called in an unnecessarily loud voice, yet in fair English, "are you lost?"

Raasleer laughed roughly. "No, we're not lost. We're taking these cattle to Zapata to sell. What do you want?"

"You are crossing my *rancho*. For that you should pay me."

Raasleer shook his head and answered in a tight voice. "This is open range. There's not a ranch within thirty miles. Let us through."

The bandit leader did not answer at once. A puzzled expression puckered his brow, then it disappeared with an almost imperceptible shrug of his shoulders. "Why are there so many *caballeros* with such a small number of cattle?" The look in his eyes said he knew the answer already.

Russ concentrated on the two Mexicans straight in front of him. The one on the left wore a heavy beard and his long unkempt hair had streaks of gray. He seemed very old still to be riding the bandit trail. The second man, wearing a dirty red shirt, was at least fifteen years younger.

Which man would be quicker with his gun? Russ decided he would try to kill the older bandit first. There must be some very good reason why he had survived so long.

Caloon's voice hissed into Russ's ear. "Remember, shoot and move; make your horse move. Mexicans usually ain't as good shots as Americans. So make yourself a moving target."

Raasleer, voice edged with warning, sounded again. "We have many riders to kill anyone who should make a mistake and try to steal our cows."

The Mexican grinned, showing big teeth, surprisingly white. "There are no bandits here. But you are on my *rancho* and for five American dollars for each one of your cows you may cross." After a slight pause the man added, "Safely."

"We have no money, even if we wanted to pay," said Raasleer.

The bandit chief straightened slightly. *"Esta muy mal"* (That is very bad), said the man. "If you have no *dinero* you may pay me as you return from Zapata. I will be waiting, *amigos*." He emphasized the last word as he reined his horse to the right.

Russ relaxed, glad the confrontation was ending without bloodshed. He twisted in the saddle to watch Raasleer.

Just in time to see the rustler leader draw and fire upon the Mexican bandit. But that shot was almost too slow, for the bandit's turning away had been a trick. Even as he reined his horse to hide his gun hand, he pulled his weapon. Raasleer's bullet tore through the man's side, driving him from the saddle.

Russ was stunned by the sudden clash of the two leaders. Then the danger to himself stung him into action. He stabbed his horse with his right spur and leaned left quickly. He plunged his hand for his revolver. Brought it up, thumbing the hammer back, squeezing the trigger.

The word *amigo* had been a signal for the attack and the older bandit had not been surprised. He fired his hand gun as Russ's pistol cleared leather.

Russ's horse, recoiling from the sharp pain of the pointed spur, snatched him from in front of the bandit's gun. The bullet tugged at Russ's shirt sleeve as it zipped past.

He busted the bandit's heart with the first shot, then threw himself forward to fall along the left side of his horse's neck. He caught the mane of the horse with his free hand, and swung his gun to line up on the younger Mexican.

That man's steed, half rearing in fright at the roar of the guns, partially hid its owner's body. Russ raised his sight to avoid hitting the horse and shot the man through the bridge of the nose, slamming him backward. He hung there, lying backward on the rump of the horse. Then his feet came loose from the stirrups and he tumbled to the ground.

Russ jerked back erect in the saddle and whirled to the left to see how his companions near him were faring in the gunfight. Caloon lay on the ground with his horse, one leg pinned beneath the heavy brute. Caloon fired over the top of the dead horse, knocking his second opponent from the saddle.

Beyond Caloon, Corddry shot twice into the center of the chest of the man opposing him. He had disposed of both his enemies. He pulled a quick, tight rein to control his gun-scared horse.

Russ swiveled his sight to check Kanttner. The man was bleeding from the side of the face, but he still sat his mount. His only adversary was down.

Through a cloud of gunpowder smoke that partly obscured his view, Russ hastily looked to the far end of the battleground. Both Gredler and Banty were sprawled on the ground, motionless. As Russ had feared, they had been greatly outnumbered and had been gunned down. They had managed to dispose of only one enemy between them.

Russ thrust out his six-gun and made a long shot past Raasleer to wound a bandit. Shot again, killing him. At the same instant, Raasleer was firing rapidly and killed another enemy, the third for him.

The nerves of the four remaining bandits broke and they spurred their horses to escape. Russ jammed his pistol into its holster and jerked his rifle out from under his leg. With one shot, he smashed the nearest bandit to the ground. He drew aim again, on a large man whipping his horse furiously, saw the v-notch and the bead-front sight line up on the center of his back, and knew with certainty he could kill this man and the other two if he wanted to.

Russ raised the sight of the rifle and blasted the man's hat from his head.

The men slunk lower in the saddles and flogged their straining ponies. Russ laughed and he sucked in a lungful of air; even with the heavy smell of gunpowder, it was goddamn sweet. He savored the glorious feeling of a battle won and still being alive.

Caloon watched Russ, seeing the willingness to fight,

more than that, the desire to do battle. The killer instinct was growing in his strong young friend. Yet hadn't he missed with the last shot on purpose, hit the hat instead of the man?

Raasleer had also observed Russ's finish of the fight. How many Mexicans had Russ killed? Three? Four? Raasleer saw the change of target to the hat. There was still a taint of softness in the young gunman, an emotion that could slow a man's gun.

In the startling quietness after the crash of six-gun and rifle, Russ let his eyes drift across the enemy's portion of the dueling ground. He counted twelve bandits slumped in awkward mounds on the ground. Three of their horses were down, caught in the fusillade of bullets.

During the five seconds of battle, he had killed four men. Every shot had gone exactly to his point of aim. He was confident he could fire again or many times with the same precision.

He twisted around to stare past Corddry at Raasleer. I must stop you before you hurt the girl. If I kill you and Corddry, the gang will fall apart. Is now the time to try and do it?

Raasleer sensed the danger to him and focused his attention on Russ. He did not blink, for Russ could draw and kill quicker than that. He held the younger man's look and recognized the fearless animal, sure of its skill.

You are very, very good with a gun, thought Raasleer. But I can still beat you. So make your play.

Corddry saw the tenseness in Raasleer and also twisted around to face Russ.

Caloon called from the ground. "Get this damn horse off me. I think it's broken my leg."

Russ hesitated, doubtful if he should take his eyes off Raasleer. It was either start the play or let it drop. If it could be dropped. And Kanttner was behind him, would shoot him in the back, for that man would take up Raasleer's fight.

Russ grinned at Raasleer and Corddry to break the tension and stepped down from his horse. He glanced at Kanttner and found him mopping at the wound on his face with a dirty neckerchief.

"That doesn't look bad, just a crease," said Russ. "Help me lift the horse off Caloon."

Kanttner pressed the cloth tightly to sop up the blood one last time, then climbed down. "A horse's weight goes from a thousand pounds to a ton the minute he dies," he growled.

Russ took a firm hold on the mane and ear of the dead animal. Kanttner moved in close to the thick body, squatted down, and positioned the front legs up under his arm.

"Get set," said Russ, "now *liiift!*"

They heaved mightily in unison and the horse rose a hand's breadth clear of the ground. Caloon pulled his leg free and sat rubbing it. "That damn Mexican shot my pony after he was dead. I had him already nailed right through the heart and he still squeezed the trigger."

Gingerly he stood up and began to hobble about, testing the injured limb. "Not broken, just bruised. I'll be good as new in a day or two."

"Good," said Russ. He loosened the cinch of Caloon's saddle and with a powerful wrench of his shoulders dragged the stirrup from under the horse.

Raasleer rode up and dismounted. "Gredler and Banty are dead, and nothing we can do for them. Let's search the Mexicans and see what they have that's worth taking."

"They look mighty poorly to me," said Caloon. "I don't expect we'll find much."

"Let's take what we want and get out of here," said Russ in a stiff voice. He was anxious to be a long distance from the smell of dead men and horses. Already the flies were starting to gather and crawl on the thickening blood.

"Some of the ponies look good," observed Kanttner.

"All right, let's get it done," said Raasleer. "Don't keep anything that can be identified. Most everything they have will be stolen. Any ponies we don't want, take the saddles off and turn them loose."

Russ stalked away to begin a quick rummage through the belongings of the four bandits he had killed. Ten minutes later he surveyed his booty. Five ten-dollar gold pieces and a handful of silver had been found. One rifle and two pistols were worth keeping. He selected the best mount of the four and put a lead rope on it.

Swinging astride his own mount, he leaned on the pommel of the saddle and watched the other men at their ghastly scavenging. The stink of death had grown worse and hung like a pall over the scene. He felt sick. He moved upwind of the stench, toward the cattle.

"That all you going to take?" called Kanttner.

Russ nodded shortly.

"Then I'm going to take that horse and saddle." He took hold of the bridle of the horse the older bandit had been riding.

"Found me a fair horse," said Caloon, riding up to Russ, "and about thirty dollars. I was right, they were a poor bunch of bastards."

" 'Bout as sorry as we are," muttered Russ.

Caloon tried to interpret his partner's meaning. "Better to kill bandits than honest men," he said.

"What we're doing is bad work and I feel like I want to puke."

"Then why in hell don't you get out of here?" flared Caloon.

In a voice iced with determination, Russ replied, "I've got two men to kill."

Caloon's anger turned to surprise. "Anyone I know?"

Russ stared into the face of his partner, a man prone to do

violence, and knew he could not tell him. Caloon was just apt to take on the job himself. Russ would tell him later.

Caloon waited for a moment, then determined he was not to be told. "I can see you're not inclined to say. So what do you plan to do after that little chore is finished?"

"I haven't thought beyond that."

Edmonton and his crew of cowboys slept on the ground in a patch of tall brush. Shallow alone was awake and he sprawled on a high, rocky point of country a hundred yards from the others. The spindly limbs and narrow leaves of a palo verde tree gave him meager shade. It was near noon and not one living thing moved; even his companions below were hidden from his view by the desert brush.

They had reached the border an hour into the day with not one track of the stolen herd having been found during the long, exhausting night of search. Somehow the rustlers had evaded them, probably during the storm, Shallow decided. He tried to calculate which direction the outlaws had turned—east, or west?—or had they holed up someplace to wait out the pursuers?

This was a big land, and the mountains, with their screening cover of brush, had a thousand secret hiding places. To a stranger it was a desolate place without water. Shallow, however, knew that within five or, at the most, ten miles in any direction he could find enough water for two hundred cows. The rustlers must also know where there were water holes. Hadn't they been driving stolen cattle across the desert for years?

There were half a score of valleys leading to Mexico between the north–south trending highlands. It would take a great amount of luck to again find the tracks of the rustlers in that maze of broken topography.

Edmonton came up the slope and squatted down beside Shallow. "Anything?"

"Nothing."

"Do you think we should divide the men and send half to the east and half to the west to try and locate the trail?" asked Edmonton.

"We could do that and sooner or later pick up sign. But half of our men couldn't take the cattle from the rustlers or even hold them until one man rode for help. Anyway, my guess is that they are already in Mexico. We've lost unless we want to go to Zapata. That's my guess as to where the heifers will be sold."

"What kind of town is this Zapata? Is it law abiding?"

"There's really two parts to Zapata. Most of it is for the Mexicans and the law is very strict. That's the south part. Now there's a north section made up of cantinas, whorehouses, and rooms for rent. This is an area of four blocks or so and is left fairly much alone for the entertainment of the *norteamericanos*. These *gringos* are mostly outlaws, killers, rustlers like we've been trailing, and general riffraff that has run there to hide or spend some stolen money on a good time."

"Will the heifers be easy to sell?"

Shallow chuckled without mirth. "The Mexicans don't like *gringos*—too many battles over the years. And they seemed to have always lost. Even an honest Mexican would buy the stock without any qualms at all. He probably would think he was getting back at the Americans for old wrongs."

"What would we do if we did find them in Zapata?"

"Nothing as long as they stayed in town. The Mexican army wouldn't allow us to start a full-scale shoot-out."

Edmonton was silent for a few moments, gazing off to the south. "We have three Mexican cowhands with us. How well do you know them? How far can they be trusted?"

Shallow smiled knowingly. "Ah, you plan to send scouts south of the border? Well, I can vouch for two of the

Mexes. They've worked on jobs with me for several years. They're some kind of relation to each other. Names are Xavier and Prim Herrera. Cousins, I think. They're damn good *pistoleros*. I've seen them in action."

"We must know exactly who the rustlers are and where the cattle are sold. Tell the men to come here and talk with me."

Shallow left and returned with two small, wiry men, both wearing black bristly mustaches. They do look related, thought Edmonton. He noted the long-barreled pistols and cartridge belts full of ammunition strapped to their waists.

"You want to talk with us, *Jefe?*" asked Xavier.

"Yes, I want you and Prim to go into Mexico. I do not plan to lose my cattle to any gang of rustlers. Every one of them must pay. Will you do it?"

"It will be very dangerous," said Xavier, "but we will go. What is it you want us to do?"

The men discussed their plans for more than half an hour. Then the two Mexican cowboys selected mounts without the Bar E brand and rode at a fast gallop to the south.

"All right, Ken, now we must tell my partner what we are doing. Send a rider to find Blackaby and ask him to have some men look after the ranch on the Gila. Also, we need supplies, enough to last at least two weeks. And more men with guns if he can spare them. I plan to catch those bloody, thieving rustlers when they come back across the border and either shoot the hell out of them or hang them."

Chapter 15

The .30-30 carbine cracked and a fist-size rock a hundred yards away exploded into fragments. Another shot and a second stone was pulverized.

Samantha lowered the rifle from her shoulder. "How was that, Grandfather?"

"Fair. Fair," responded Lafe Tamblin. "But you took a mite long to get your gun on the target. Now try it again. Line your sights as the gun comes up, not down, for that blocks your view of what you want to hit. And don't hesitate; the second the sights are on, squeeze the trigger."

"The rifle kicks a little," said Sam.

Lafe chuckled. "Soon you won't feel that. You'll be able to shoot a cannon from your shoulder."

"I doubt that. But I'll shoot some more. I want to become an expert marksman."

They stood in the front yard of the cabin near the spring. Several small rocks had been placed on top of a large boulder at a reasonable distance for practice. The sun was behind Sam and the line of fire was down the valley.

She shot rapidly three times. Two were direct hits,

smashing the rocks. The third was a glancing blow, flipping the rock into the brush.

"Good," said Lafe.

Sam acknowledged the compliment with a quick smile at him. She was proud of her skill with the rifle. Over the past few days she had practiced more than all the time before. Her handling of the .32 caliber-pistol, which she now wore almost all the time, was only passable. Yet, even with that weapon, she felt the clumsiness leaving her hand.

"Let's stop for today, Grandfather," she said. As she reloaded the rifle, her eyes flicked up toward the crest of the mountain.

Lafe watched his granddaughter's face. Ever since she had ridden hurriedly to tell him and her father of the warning of the strange young man on Growler Mountain, she had been quiet and seldom smiled or laughed. She had little interest in things around her, except for the daily gun practice and a careful watchfulness of the surrounding land.

Lafe thought he recognized the symptoms, but was not yet certain how serious the disease was.

"Do you think it would be safe for me to ride up to the pass?" asked Sam.

"No, I'm afraid not and neither your father nor I have time to go up with you."

Sam pivoted to look directly at Lafe with bright yet self-conscious eyes. "I want to see him again—very much. Is that wrong?"

"No, Samantha, that's a womanly feeling and perfectly proper."

She liked for him to use her full name at this time. He had started it very recently when the subject they discussed concerned her growing-up emotions. She examined the deep creases in his face and the pale blue, caring eyes. He was easy to talk with.

"Will I ever see him again?"

"If he's halfway smart and has an eye for a pretty young woman, he'll be back."

"I'm not sure, Grandfather. He acted as if he had a long distance to travel."

"What kind of a fellow was he?"

"He looked very strong and sure of himself. But he seemed like a gentle man. What do you suppose he was doing on the mountain?"

"Warning us for one thing. And he was correct, too, for I've seen sign of horses. Whoever the riders are, they've been on the ridge tops watching us. We must stay on our guard."

"I hope Dad is safe."

"If anyone can take care of himself, your dad can. Somebody has to check the cows and keep the water holes open. And he said he found some wolf tracks around a dead cow. Maybe he can get a shot at it, but they're cautious animals and few are happened upon. Now let's go do some irrigating. This hot weather sure causes the meadow grass to use a lot of water."

The four rustlers sat around the table in the cantina and drank cold beer. All night long the keg of brew had lain in the water at the bottom of the deep well behind the building. Now it rested in a place of honor in a wooden rack on the center of the bar. A thick cotton blanket, wet and dripping onto the earthen floor, hung draped across the cask, prolonging its delicious coolness.

"Another drink all 'round," Corddry called to the barman and owner.

"God, that's good drink," said Kanttner. "Someone in this town sure knows how to brew beer."

Caloon nodded his head in agreement. He was in a mellow mood. "How do you know if it was made here?"

"Berdugo told me," said Kanttner.

Corddry chuckled. "Then we shouldn't have to worry about drinking all the kegs dry."

Russ savored a mug of the beverage. He had had little alcohol to drink in his life to compare this against, but he agreed with Kanttner that it had an excellent flavor.

It was the morning of the third day since the shoot-out with the bandits. Berdugo had met the bone-weary men yesterday on the outskirts of Zapata. He was well known here and had acquired pasture from a friend. The exhausted heifers were left there to recuperate from the long forced drive while the men continued on into town.

On Berdugo's advice, the men rented rooms above the cantina and, hardly taking time to pull off their boots and clothing, threw their grimy bodies into the soft beds. Raasleer instructed Berdugo to keep a lookout for the Englishman and other possible danger. Knowing this, all the other members of the rustler band slept the evening and night away. Not once did they hear the noisy rowdiness from the bar below.

Russ arose remarkably refreshed and with no effect from the long, hard ride. He found a bathhouse; while he leisurely soaked the dirt away, the attendant washed his clothing. They were dried and ironed by the time he finished.

Caloon came in as Russ left. "Raasleer's out selling the cows. Said for us all to meet him in the saloon after dinner."

"All right," said Russ. "I'm going to get a shave. I'll see you there later on.

With his stomach full and the beer pleasant in his mouth, Russ leaned his back against the wall and viewed his surroundings. The cantina was large with a long, wooden bar and about twenty tables. Russ judged seventy or so customers could be served at one time. Besides his own crew, there were three old Mexican men near the open front door.

At the far end of the bar and beyond a swinging door was the restaurant that had supplied the food for their noon meal. The aroma of refried pinto beans, baking corn bread, and the tanginess of chili peppers drifted to Russ as he sat relaxed. It was good to be off the desert and back in civilization for a spell.

Raasleer and Berdugo came in from the street through the open door with their spurs jingling and wide smiles on their faces. Raasleer carried a leather pouch and he lifted it up to let it drop into his outstretched hand. The dull metal clink of gold coins came to the four men at the table.

Both men pulled up chairs and sat down. Raasleer spoke, pleased with himself. "We got a very good price. We finally agreed on thirty-one dollars a head for the heifers. Could have gotten another four or five if we waited until they had gotten back into condition. Several were lame."

Four Americans, armed with pistols on their hips, came into the cantina and bellied up to the bar to order drinks. Raasleer and Caloon were facing that direction and both shifted their views to look the men over. The new arrivals appeared not to notice the men at the table.

The rustler leader spoke in a low voice. "One hundred eighty animals at thirty-one dollars each. My three shares, Corddry's two, all the rest of you one apiece, including the two men taking care of the cows back at camp. That's eleven shares."

He looked at Caloon and Russ. "You've both earned a full share since you were in all the way on stealing these cows."

The two men nodded.

Raasleer continued to speak. "First off, we take out one hundred dollars American for the local Mexican law so we won't be bothered by questions." Raasleer set that quantity aside and then methodically began to count out each man's portion of what was left into a neat pile. When he finished, he rebagged his gold, along with that belonging to the two men in the Kofas, for later division.

Russ raked his pile of coins, $498 in gold, into his hand and shoved them into a pocket. He stood up, preparing to leave.

"Wait," said Raasleer, "I want to buy all of you a drink of the best whiskey in the house." He waved a hand at the bar owner. "Bring a bottle of your best."

Russ reseated himself and watched the bartender spin six shot glasses around the table and pour them brimfull with amber liquid.

"Here's to a job well done." Raasleer raised his glass.

Caloon caught Russ's eye, the look saying, "At least the son of a bitch is correct about that." And they lifted their drinks with the others and downed them with a gulp.

The flame of the liquid seared Russ's throat, the fumes burned his nostrils. The beer had been good; he had expected the whiskey to be also. The harsh, rasping passage of it down into his gullet proved him painfully wrong.

He held his face steady, kept the tears out of his eyes. The heat passed and he stood up. He touched the edge of his hat to the men he had fought a battle with and strode from the cantina.

A feeling of success excited Russ. In less than a week he had earned a man's yearly salary and he was safely in Mexico with it. Then, just as rapidly as the wonderful sensation had arrived, it faded away.

He was still a murderer. The gold hanging heavily against his leg had come from the sale of stolen cattle. Honest men would want nothing to do with him. The girl of the Growlers would spit in his face if he dared approach her as an equal.

He turned away from those thoughts and surveyed the town of Zapata spread before him. It was larger than he had expected, perhaps with a population nigh a thousand, and very prosperous appearing.

A medium-size stream wound through the center of town. The main street followed along beside it. Lining the thoroughfare were many places of business. There was a superabundance of cantinas, all concentrated on the north end of the street. The town had many homes. Small adobes of the peons bordered the streets. Very prestigious residences were located on the higher bench where more cooling winds blew.

He noticed the wide main street had been graveled to control the mud when it rained. A sign before a new building under construction caught his attention. Using his knowledge of Spanish, learned from his father, who was fluent in the language, Russ made out the words: a hardware and farm supply store would soon be open for business there.

Russ was surprised at the need for so large a structure for that purpose. He looked beyond the town limits. On both sides of the stream and as far away as he could see, lay irrigated farmland.

He turned back to the livery stable, saddled his roan horse, and rode out into the cultivated bottomland. As he moved along, he mentally calculated the acres being cropped and judged there must be three to four thousand.

A road angled off to the west and climbed up to the first bench level above the flood plain. Wanting to get a better view of the surprisingly large irrigation system, Russ guided the horse onto the road. He touched the horse with his spurs and the animal broke into a lope.

At the top of the grade, Russ halted to look down. The watered fields were startlingly green against the dark brown of the desert. On the upper edge of each plot of land ran an irrigation ditch. Here and there men were in the fields keeping the corrugations open or removing weeds. Most of the crops were hay; however, vegetables and orchards of apples and pears were also common. Some of the trees were very large. The people had lived here many years. Mexico was an old country. Russ wished he had one of the farms and the peace that went with it.

From a short distance away an old woman's voice, calling a warning in Spanish, startled Russ out of his reverie.

"Manuel, that horse will kill you. Your old bones will break when he throws you on the ground."

"Woman, I have tamed a thousand mustangs in my day. What is one more?"

Russ examined the house off to his right, and the small wooden corral near it. He saw movement between the railings and then a rapidly bobbing head as a rider was bucked around the enclosure. The head suddenly vanished. The old woman screamed.

The roan leaped into life at Russ's sharp command and rushed up to slide to a stop at the corral. Russ went up and over the horizontal poles. And down inside to see the mustang still bucking, trying to throw the empty saddle.

The horse came around, its flying heels hurling large clods of dirt, and bore down on the old Mexican sitting groggily on the ground. Russ sprang forward. With all his strength he slapped the horse along the side of its head with his big hat, deflecting the wild beast a foot from the thrown rider.

He hoisted the man to his feet and shuffled him rapidly through the gate to the outside.

"*Muchas gracias, mi joven amigo*" (Many thanks, my young friend), said the man and leaned on the poles of the corral.

"*De nada*, grandfather," replied Russ. "Are you hurt?"

"No, only slightly dizzy."

The woman hurried up. "You silly old man. I told you not to try that."

"Enough, woman. Everything is all right now. You should be telling this new friend how much you appreciate that I am still alive."

She turned large brown eyes, the fear and dread just fading from them, on Russ. "The old bandit is all I have in the world." She reached out to stroke the man's veined hand. "Thank you for keeping him safe."

Russ smiled at her and turned back to the man. "Do you want me to take the fire out of the horse for you?"

"Ah, that would be much appreciated," said the man, very much pleased.

Picking up a lasso from where it hung on one of the uprights of the gate, Russ went back inside the corral. The horse had ceased its frantic bucking and stood breathing deeply at the far side of the pen. Its wild eyes never left the man as he closed in.

The lasso flew true over the animal's head and settled around the long neck. Instantly the horse charged away. Russ ran with him, holding firmly to the end of the rope. As he passed the snubbing post set in the center of the corral, he took a hasty turn of the lasso around it.

The mustang hit the end of the rope and swapped ends in a cloud of dust. He went halfway to his knees and struggled not to go all the way down.

Russ loosened the rope from the post and dashed up to lunge into the saddle. His sudden weight almost toppled the horse. As the animal caught his balance and came fully to his feet, Russ flipped the noose from his head.

Then all hell broke loose as the mustang went into a paroxysm of bucks. For the next two minutes, the man and horse warred against each other.

To Russ it was a whirligig of violent spins, of ups and downs. He thought his arm would break with the pressure he kept on the reins to pull the animal's head up and lessen his ability to buck.

He rode the mustang to a trembling, straddle-legged stop. Then he spurred him into a slow walk around the enclosure. He pulled the animal to a stop, only to make him move again. Finally Russ swung down.

"*Magnifico, magnifico!*" called the man. "Do not unsaddle him. I will ride him every hour while he is still tired. I will ride him until he knows who is the master. Come inside and wash up. We will have something to drink."

The adobe house was cool, with shadows in the corners. The furnishings were simple, yet neat and clean. The two men found seats in a large, sunken living room and the woman promptly served them wine in silver goblets. Russ was surprised at the presence of the precious metal. The overall appearance of prosperity of the house did not indicate such wealth.

"He truly was a bandit," said the woman, seeing Russ evaluating the silver articles. "But then one day he came into this valley and did not leave again."

The man smiled and nodded. "The only thing of value I possessed were six silver goblets I had stolen from"—he paused, looking a little embarrassed—"an American. Then I stole her and had two things of worth. I borrowed against the silver to buy this land—sixty acres, forty irrigated and twenty above the canal. Over the next thirty years I repaid the loan. Now my wife lets only her true friends drink from her silver treasures."

"I am honored," said Russ, much impressed with their kindness.

They talked of many things during the remainder of the day. Russ learned the town was more than eighty years old. That the river flooded, on the average, one in six years. And, on average again, there was one killing each five days. Almost all the dead were *gringos*.

He also learned that a bandit could become an honest man

if he sincerely wanted to. At dusk the woman served a bountiful meal.

Russ spent the night there, resting under a thin mosquito netting for the insects were plentiful along the irrigation canals. A pleasant breeze wafted through an open window to keep him cool all night.

At first light of dawn, he arose and returned directly to Zapata. He must always watch Raasleer so he could not send violent men to the Growler Mountains without his knowing.

Chapter 16

Caloon and Russ were at the smithy having the old shoes removed from the hooves of their four horses and new iron tacked into place. Caloon had kept the horse taken from the bandits, finding it a sound animal. Russ had sold the one he had acquired.

They stood outside the big open door, watching the people on the street. Caloon said, "Raasleer has taken four new men into the gang. Those *hombres* that came into the cantina yesterday while we were splitting up the money."

"I suppose he figures he needs some new hands. He's lost several in the past week or so," said Russ. "Those fellows looked plenty tough."

"We'll see how rough they are later on. Several of us are going to have a poker game this evening. Do you want to join in?"

"Yes, I think so. As long as the stakes aren't too high."

Caloon jingled the coins in his pocket. "I want them high. I plan to win. Don't forget what I said about getting a ranch. With luck, two years from now I'll have enough money to buy a small one."

"I've heard big stakes make men ornery," said Russ.

"The betting always gets larger as the game wears on, but you can drop out whenever you want."

Caloon stuck his head inside the blacksmith shop and called out, *"Estan listos los caballos?"*

"I am finished now," answered the smith. "You can take your horses."

They paid the man and, after returning the horses to the livery, walked to the cantina. The card game, five-card stud, was already in progress. Raasleer, Corddry, and the new men were playing.

Russ and Caloon took seats on opposite sides of the table. The cantina owner, acting as the banker, gave them chips for gold coins. He took a cut of a dollar from each man for the house.

Introductions were made. Speegle was a large man, slow of speech. Steen was tall, with a large domed head, mostly bald. A third man, called Walt, was a nondescript individual that no one would remember tomorrow. Dazell was slim and nervous. He had been the leader of the band before they joined Raasleer. During the game, as Russ watched Dazell's quick hands deal the cards with great skill, he wondered how good the man would be with a gun.

By ten o'clock the cantina was full of patrons and stuffy with smoke and voices at a low roar. Seven or eight dark-skinned young women mixed with the customers, talking them into buying drinks, now and then enticing one of the men into a back room.

Russ was more than a hundred-dollar winner. He was playing conservatively, folding on weak hands and betting hard on good ones. He knew the other players were waiting for him to try a bluff. Maybe he would soon.

Caloon was ahead slightly. Raasleer was also winning by several dollars. Speegle and Dazell were losers. Walt and Steen, heavy losers, had quit the game earlier.

Russ had observed the increasing tenseness of the two new men. From the look they exchanged, Russ judged they suspected their recently acquired comrades of cheating. Russ thought it time to quit. He tossed his cards onto the table and began to count his chips.

Berdugo sidled up through the crowd and said something to Raasleer in a low voice. Raasleer asked a question and Berdugo nodded at the two small Mexicans at the bar. The rustler leader's eyes swept around to lock onto the men. "Are you sure?" he questioned.

Berdugo answered in a voice loud enough for Russ to hear. "They've been asking questions about us and where we sold the heifers. I asked some questions myself and found out they used to ride for Blackaby. I believe they work for the Englishman now."

Raasleer studied the men, his face hard. "Do you know what kind of horses they own?"

"Good horses. A dun and a sorrel."

"Any brands?"

Berdugo thought for a moment. "No, I didn't see any."

Raasleer grinned wolfishly. "All right. They know what we look like. So we must make sure they don't return to the Territory. Back my play if I need it." He loosened his six-gun in its holster and rose up from the table.

The Mexicans had been watching the reflection in the long bar mirror and had seen the exchange of words and the hostile looks cast in their direction. Unhurriedly they turned and began to make their way through the crowd toward the door into the restaurant.

"Wait, you two!" cried Raasleer in a harsh, challenging voice. "You're the ones that stole my horses."

The men flinched at the sharp command, but continued to move away.

"Goddamn you, *halta usted*" (stop, I say) "or I will shoot you in the back."

Russ saw the spines of the two men stiffen, but their leisurely amble in the direction of the exit did not waver.

Raasleer snatched up a beer mug from the table and hurled it at the cowboys. It passed between them and smashed with a shower of glass against the wall of the restaurant.

The small dark men pivoted, stepping away from each other and facing Raasleer.

"You are speaking to us?" asked Xavier in a level voice.

"You know I am, you damn horse thief."

"We are not thieves. We steal nothing," said Prim. The faces of the men were tense, but showed no fear.

Other customers of the cantina standing near, heard the fighting words and saw the preparation for gun play. They hastily moved back, leaving the two cowboys standing by themselves and facing the big *gringos* at the table.

Russ watched the Englishman's cowhands. The large mustaches looked oversized on their thin, tight faces. They had courage. Yet they were dead men and must know it. Russ felt pity for them. No way could they beat the guns of six rustlers.

No, not six pistols, decided Russ. He would not help Raasleer.

"I say that dun and sorrel you ride are mine. For stealing them you are going to die." Raasleer's voice was merciless.

The two cowboys drew their six-guns very swiftly. Yet Raasleer's hand was faster. He shot the man on the left first, staggering him backward, his falling body crashing into the wall of the cantina. The man fired his gun into the floor at his feet as his hand convulsed in death on the trigger.

The second cowboy lunged to his left and tried to bring his gun in alignment on Raasleer. He was too slow. The rustler chief's bullet tore a hole in his shoulder, spinning him half around to face the front wall of the cantina.

In a desperate effort to escape certain death, the man

hurled himself through the nearest window in the wall. In a crash of sash and glass, he disappeared into the darkness outside. His pistol clattered to the floor of the cantina.

"Catch him!" yelled Raasleer, whipping his hand past his men and pointing to the broken window. "Outside. Kill him. He mustn't escape."

Russ rushed to the street with the other gang members. All, except Russ, carried their six-guns in their hands, even Caloon.

There was no sign of the man in the dim lamplight spilling from the windows onto the wooden sidewalk.

"Check the alley," commanded Raasleer, motioning to Speegle and Russ, who stood nearest.

Speegle immediately dashed to the opening of the alley. He stopped and peered cautiously into the blackness. Russ came up behind him.

"He doesn't have a gun, get him," ordered Raasleer.

Russ and Speegle entered the alley with guns drawn. Russ hoped he would not be forced into a situation where he would have to shoot the Mexican. Behind them he heard Raasleer sending men off in other directions.

Light from a window at the far end of the alley allowed Russ to see a little. He counted seven or eight back doors. All were closed. A large number of beer kegs were piled close to the rear entrance of the cantina.

"I'll look behind the kegs," said Russ.

In the soft dust his footfalls were noiseless. He stretched up to peer over the kegs. Russ heard the cowboy catch his breath as they came face to face.

"Por favor" (Please), whispered the man in a desperate voice.

Russ glanced to see where Speegle was. Found him trying doors along the alley.

"Nothing here," called Russ. He turned to follow after Speegle.

Half an hour later all of the rustler gang had regathered in the cantina. The cowboy had not been found.

Raasleer said, "No chance for a bunch of Americans to find a Mex in a Mex town. Nobody is going to help us. Berdugo will take some of his friends and see what he can find. The rest of you can go do what you want. Corddry, you stay with me. If Berdugo needs help, you and I will give him some."

Russ went to his room. He propped a chair under the doorknob and sat on the bed to pull off his boots. If Raasleer found out he had seen the cowboy and then let him escape, there would be hell to pay.

Without taking off his clothes, Russ lay down and tried to rest. Twice during the night he heard pistol shots. Each time he wondered if the cowboy had been killed. He did not go to investigate; there was nothing more he could do.

Russ did not sleep well and he went down to the restaurant for an early breakfast. Raasleer, Corddry, and two of the new men, Dazell and Steen, sat eating together.

Raasleer noticed Russ and motioned for him to join them. "Just the fellow I wanted to see. I'm sending these men up north to the Growler Mountains to find out if there really is a new ranch there. If the rumors are true, I want you men to make sure they leave. One way or the other. Just leave the cattle there and we'll gather them later.

"I want you to go with them. You know where the water is. The ranch will be at one of the springs. Try that big spring on the northeast side first."

"Suits me to go," said Russ. "I'm ready to leave right now. Do we come back down here?"

"No," said Raasleer. "We'll all be leaving sometime today, too. We're cutting this visit short. You men go on to the Kofas after you finish on the Growlers." He looked at Corddry. "I'll move the hideout to Rattlesnake Canyon soon as I get back. Don't let the Englishman see you or trail you there. Since he had his men here in Zapata, that means he's out there waiting for us."

"Don't worry about the Englishman," said Corddry. "He won't see hide nor hair of us."

"Did you catch his cowboy?" asked Russ.

"Nope, just plumb vanished," said Raasleer.

A pretty girl came and took Russ's order for breakfast. She examined the fair *norteamericano* with interest. This particular group of men had many gold pieces from the sale of stolen cattle. She wondered if she could interest this young one. Her thigh touched his arm as she placed his food before him.

Russ ignored the girl and ate quickly. He left the restaurant with the other men. Twenty minutes later the four had their bedrolls tied behind their saddles and, leading a spare horse apiece, rode from the town.

The men and horses were fresh and they traveled swiftly. By dusk they had passed the south end of the Growlers and were a substantial distance along their east flank. Ajo Mountain was on the far horizon to the northeast. The wide flat valley of the Ajo lay to their right. They had seen no sign of the Englishman.

They found no water, so made a dry camp. With little talk, beds were unrolled and the men flopped down. Russ rested off by himself, his horse near and his guns close to his hand. Tomorrow he would find water for the animals.

Russ was anxious to see the girl again. But not under these circumstances. Yet he had to go with the men to try to prevent them from harming her. He had made himself her protector and did not even know her name. He laughed at himself. Still, he knew the self-imposed task was very important to him.

The moon came up and spilled light down through a hole

in a high thin layer of clouds. Wind rattled the brittle brush nearby. On the mountain above the camp, a red desert wolf howled, wild and lonely, a weird and lovely sound. For a moment Russ savored the call of the savage brute. Then he pictured the beautiful face of the girl of the mountain and drifted off into a light sleep.

Lafe and Samantha dug postholes for the fence that would soon be completed to surround the irrigated meadow along the creek. A few head of cows had strayed down from where they had been driven on the upper pastures of the Growler. Once the animals tasted the sweet meadow grass, they did not want to return to the steep slopes of the mountain. More would follow; the fence was needed to protect the hayfield for cutting as a feed supply when winter snow covered the land.

Sam heard the drum of hoofbeats when the four riders came out from behind the point of the hill to the south. They came at a steady trot, miniature men on miniature horses, riding abreast, weaving through the desert brush. As she examined them, they grew rapidly in size.

"Grandfather, men are coming," called Sam, and dropped her shovel to come and stand close to him.

Lafe, cursing his failing hearing, shaded his eyes and scrutinized the horsemen. Each led a spare mount, meaning they must always be able to travel long distances with certainty. They came from the direction of Mexico, and thus were not at all likely to be some of Blackaby's cowhands. A prickle of alarm touched his spine.

"Go get your rifle and come back here. Hurry!" Lafe ordered Samantha.

"I've got my pistol," said Samantha.

"This is no damn time for toys," said Lafe, thinking of the .32-caliber gun. "Get the rifle." He touched the butt of his six-gun and watched the approaching men.

"I have it," said Sam, coming up by his side.

Lafe turned and took hold of her shoulders and gripped her firmly, hurting her a little. "I don't like the looks of this. I think they mean trouble. You go over behind that boulder and stay out of sight. If I touch my nose or start shooting, I want you to shoot the man closest to you. And keep on shooting 'til they're all dead."

Sam tried to draw back from the cold blue eyes of the man. Never in her life had she seen such a fierce expression.

He held her and shook her twice, not gently. "Hear me, daughter. These men may try to kill me and do worse to you. You must help me. Don't fail me now. Aim for the center of their chest. You must do it. You must!"

Sam's heart felt constricted. The rifle in her hand was a heavy lead weight. This was not to be target practice. She tore her eyes from her grandfather's strained face.

"Now get over back of that rock. Lever a cartridge in and get ready to shoot." He shoved her away toward the black lava boulder.

The horsemen came in fast, seeming intent on riding Lafe down. He knew they were trying to scare him. He squared his shoulders and put his hand on his pistol. He would shoot the first man that came within easy range.

Corddry saw the surefire intention of the old man to stand his ground. He stopped his horse with a hard pull and stared with hostile eyes.

Russ rode in more slowly and took up position on Corddry's left. He looked at the boulder where the second person had run as they rode in. The girl watched them, just her head showing. Russ had expected to see her, yet her sudden presence caused his heart to pound. He hoped fervently she would not recognize him. He tipped his head to the side so the wide brim of his hat hid part of his face.

Lafe stood with his head thrust forward defiantly, his

mouth clamped tight. His alert eyes saw all the men, but his attention was centered on Corddry.

"Looks like you're building a nice spread here," said Corddry.

"Yep," said Lafe.

"What's your name?"

"Tamblin."

"Well, Tamblin, too bad this land is already taken. Lot of work gone for nothing.".

"Wasn't claimed until we took it up," said Lafe belligerently.

"Yes it was. Been used for years now by me and my friends. So I got to ask you to leave."

Lafe spat in the dust. "Don't plan to go anywhere. The land's ours."

"Just to be neighborly, I'll give you one hundred dollars for your cattle and everything."

"Neighborly, bullshit!" cursed Tamblin. "You're a robber if that's all you think our place is worth."

"It's either that or a shallow grave," warned Corddry.

"I still say bullshit to you, mister. And I think you should know my son with a rifle is over there behind that rock."

"We saw him plain enough. But there's four of us." It looked like a kid in the rock, and that did not bother Corddry much.

Russ tightened the rein on his horse and the beast began to back up slowly, a step at a time. Corddry noted the movement and, believing Russ was not to be trusted, grew concerned. But Corddry did not take his sight from the angry eyes of Tamblin. That decrepit old coyote seemed willing to fight them all.

Lafe saw the gunman on the right pulling back. He almost glanced that direction. Goddamn them, were they going to spread out on him? Should he touch his nose?

Would Sam shoot? If she did that would take them off guard and he could kill one, maybe two of them.

Russ was now far enough to the rear to see the backs of all three outlaws. Dazell turned toward him, suspicious. Russ stared back, keeping his face flat and emotionless. He thought, You sure as hell had better worry which side I'm going to be on if shooting starts.

The silence was broken by the sharp tattoo of a running horse. Dan Tamblin charged in to bring his mount to a sliding stop beside his father.

Lafe Tamblin grinned wickedly. "Now there's three Tamblins. That's worth four of anybody else."

Corddry was caught between the two men facing him, the kid threatening from the rocks, and the unknown intention of Russ behind. Corddry did not like the odds.

"I'll give you a week to get out of the Growler Mountains," said Corddry. "Take your livestock and leave."

"Let's kill them, Dan," whispered Lafe from the corner of his mouth. "If we let them leave they'll shoot us from ambush later."

"No, let them go. Sam's in danger. Watch close for they may turn back on us."

Corddry whirled his horse and spurred away. The others followed with Russ bringing up the rear.

In the rocks, Samantha lowered the hammer on her rifle with trembling hands and watched the outlaws ride away. She paid special attention to the straight, broad back of the young outlaw. A tear trickled down her cheek.

Chapter 17

Corddry seethed with anger. He had backed down from a fight in front of Dazell and Steen. And the reason for that was the man Russ. Goddamn his treacherous hide.

For a brief moment Corddry considered riding off a distance and then sneaking back and shooting the Tamblins without warning. He cast a look at Russ in the rear. That man was watching him with a threatening eye.

If the man was not going to back the actions of the rest of the gang, why was he still trailing along? Why not pull out and go his own way? Corddry considered the questions. No answers came. He made his plan. I'll kill you the first time I catch you off guard or sleeping.

The rustlers halted long enough at the spring near the cabin to water the horses and fill their canteens. Then they crossed up and over Growler and down into the valley on the west.

Russ did not trust Corddry. He held the tail end position on the narrow trails. When they spread out to ride the flat land, he kept Dazell and Steen between himself and Raasleer's right-hand man. The back shooter.

When the group of men entered a broad gravelly area with a steep-sided arroyo cutting through, Corddry slowed and reined sideways as if searching for a way to cross. Russ marked the change, one that would put Corddry behind him. He halted, pushed his hat to the back of his head, and pulled out a bandana to mop the sweat from his forehead. He held himself alert, wary of Corddry's intention.

Dazell had observed the jockeying for position between the two men for several hours now. He was growing annoyed by it. A sudden shoot-out betwixt them could catch him in the middle. Quite deliberately, he turned his mount and faced them, concentrating mostly on Russ.

Steen had also noticed the byplay between Corddry and Russ, and he turned with Dazell, ready to back his hand.

Russ nonchalantly repocketed his bandana with his left hand. Corddry knew where the new hideout was, where Caloon could be found. And Russ wanted to find his partner and get him away to safety before Corddry talked with Raasleer. Once the rustler chief heard that Russ had prevented the killing of the rancher, all the gang would be against Caloon. For hadn't Caloon said he would be responsible for Russ's actions?

But there was another way to protect his friend. Kill these three, if he could, before they returned to camp.

He measured Dazell. The man was an unknown. How fast was he with a six-gun? Faster than Steen, Russ felt certain.

Dazell stared back, showing no fear, only annoyance. Russ glanced at Steen very briefly. He would leave the man for last if a gunfight started.

Russ grinned at Corddry, his eyes boring in like augers. "Well, Corddry, do you have something to say to me?" Russ's voice rang.

Corddry struggled not to show his dread of having to draw against Russ. He knew the swift sureness of the gun threatening him. He studiously kept his hand away from his pistol. His furtive eyes slid away.

Dazell saw Corddry blanch beneath his tan. Why was he so afraid of this fellow, hardly a man? Then Russ's daring eyes probed at Dazell.

"Are you taking up Corddry's argument against me, Dazell?"

Before Dazell could respond, Corddry called out in a taut voice. "Let's get on to the hideout."

He knew that if those two fought, there would be no way to stop the battle until either Russ or the three of them were dead. Corddry thought he could very likely be the first target of Russ's gun. He spurred his mustang down into the arroyo. Dazell shrugged and wheeled his mount after Corddry. Steen fell next in line.

Camp was made on the flat floor of the desert fifteen miles from the Kofas. Russ sat on his bedroll and ate by himself. The other three men avoided him.

Dusk settled in and Russ lay down to rest. Later when it grew dark, he silently gathered up his blankets and slipped into the blackness along a route memorized while there was still light. A hundred feet away, among cholla cactus with their thousands of needle thorns, he again spread his bed to sleep. No one could reach him in the darkness without his hearing them.

Sometime during the night, he heard a man stumble into something and curse in pain. Then there was whispering, and finally all was quiet.

Russ arose before the sun gave the slightest hint of light in the sky. His gear was quickly packed and a horse saddled.

The others heard him moving about and awoke. At once they prepared to leave. They chewed on dried meat and fruit as they traveled. The sun came up and dissolved the shadows, exposing the towering bulk of the Kofas close on the northwest.

The four riders climbed the lower flank of the mountain. Russ noted the course was three miles south of where it would have been had they returned to the old camp. He checked the steep, broken terrain ahead and made a guess as to where the hideout would most probably be.

An hour later, after passing one lookout, they found the camp. The horses were blowing hard, for Corddry had set a fast pace.

Several members of the gang lounged about in the shade of some stunted juniper near the horse remuda. Caloon sat off by himself, propped against the bole of a tree.

Corddry stopped near Berdugo. "Where's Raasleer?" he asked.

"Him and Kanttner just rode out that way." The Mexican pointed around the side of the mountain.

Corddry left immediately in the direction indicated. Russ watched him and knew he had little time to get Caloon and himself away to safety. Corddry would report to Raasleer and that man would straightaway take action against them.

Russ dismounted beside Caloon. "Talk low," he said in a hushed voice. "Where are your horses?"

Caloon looked up quizzically. "Over there grazing," he said, and chucked a thumb at a grassy area surrounded on three sides by ragged fingers of juniper.

"Damn, that's a long ways," said Russ, mentally measuring the thousand feet or so to the pasture. Then he returned his sight to Caloon. "Now Raasleer will be trying to kill us in a few minutes, quick as Corddry can catch him and bring him back. Grab your saddle and let's get over there and catch your fresh horses. Raasleer can catch us if we ride these tired ones."

Russ stepped off, leading his two mounts. Caloon

climbed to his feet, slung his saddle over his shoulder and, taking long steps to catch up, fell in beside his partner. Dazell saw them leave and began to speak to the other men.

"What happened that Raasleer would want to kill us anymore than he already does?" asked Caloon.

"I wouldn't help them kill the rancher and they are damn mad about it," said Russ, wondering what Caloon would have done had he been there.

"You're not cut out to be a rustler," said Caloon.

"Neither one of us should be. Not even you."

"Don't be too sure about that."

"Raasleer will kill you for what I did if you stay here," said Russ.

"I think he'd like an excuse to gun me," Caloon agreed.

They entered the lower end of the grassy area. The mustangs had drifted apart and were grazing on the upper end of the clearing.

"You take the pony on the left; he's easier to catch," said Caloon.

"Are they hobbled?" asked Russ.

"Yes. Both are."

Russ knew a tinge of panic. Everything was going wrong, taking precious time they could not spare. The whole outlaw gang would soon be organized against them. Ten guns could not be beaten.

"Hurry!" said Russ. He dropped the reins of his horses and moved swiftly up the slope toward the nearest animal.

Caloon dumped the heavy saddle and struck off after the far mount.

Raasleer, followed by Corddry and Kanttner, sped into camp. With a commanding swing of his long arm, he called all the men around him.

"Where is Caloon and the kid?" Raasleer spoke hard and fast.

Berdugo answered. "They went off that way with Caloon carrying his saddle."

Raasleer looked, saw Caloon and Russ in the opening, far from cover. He smiled grimly. "Those two are plain trouble. Have been since the day they came. And now it looks like their luck has plumb run out."

He faced his men. "Corddry, Kanttner, and Jones—you're all good with a rifle. And you, Dazell, are you good with a long gun?"

"He's one of the best," volunteered Speegle.

"Good," said Raasleer. "You four take your rifles and go kill those two. Shoot them while they're out there with no place to hide. Split up into pairs, two of you on one of them. Shoot from a distance long enough they can't hit you with their six-guns."

"What about the rest of you?" asked Corddry.

"We'll go take care of the rancher in the Growlers. We'll round up his cows and take them to Mexico. The four of you, when you finish with Caloon and his sidekick, herd up all the cows we have stashed away and drive them to Mexico, too. Now the Englishman may still be out there some place near the border, so drive west for two days then go south in a big looping curve to Zapata."

Corddry was skeptical about trying to kill Caloon and his partner. "Why don't you help us shoot those two men?"

Raasleer shook his head. "If all of us try to slip up on them, we'll be spotted and they'll know something is up. Are you afraid, Corddry?"

Dazell spoke, not liking Corddry's whining. "We can shoot them easy. Just sit back a couple of hundred yards and blast the hell out of them. Now let's go get it done."

"Just to make you feel better, I'll wait until it's over," said Raasleer to Corddry. "The rest of you men pack for a fast trip to the Growlers. It'll be nearly dark when we get there. We'll catch them off guard at supper and afterward we'll sleep in their soft beds. Maybe they have women and then it'll be an interesting night."

Chuckling, the men hastened to pack and saddle.

Caloon walked toward the horse busily grazing on the mountain grass about a hundred yards up the hill from him. He let his eyes range to the left to see how Russ was doing catching the pony on the opposite side of the meadow.

A flicker of something moving in the evergreens beyond Russ caught Caloon's attention. It disappeared, then showed again, two men slipping from juniper to juniper. They were stalking Russ, only a short rifle shot distant.

A sudden alarming thought caused Caloon to spin to the rear. Yes, two men were just fading into the trees after crossing the lower end of the clearing. They carried rifles. They were after him.

Caloon cursed himself for having left his long gun with the saddle. Still, he was confident he could make the juniper, barely a hundred yards to his right. Once there, his chances for survival would be good; a pistol was almost as effective, under cover, as a rifle.

He prepared to run for it. First a shout of warning to his partner. He turned to call out.

The two men he had seen earlier were kneeling in the edge of the juniper and aiming with their rifles. Russ was still oblivious of the impending attack.

Caloon knew it was too late to yell out and explain the danger. And he knew he should be racing this very minute for the safety of the evergreen thicket. But Russ was a dead man if he was not alerted instantly. Caloon drew and fired, low and in front of his *amigo*.

Russ heard the shot, saw the ground explode in a geyser of dust and gravel not a yard ahead. By reflex he hurled himself to the dirt and rolled toward a sunken place in the earth.

The crash of rifles ripped across the mountainside. Bullets slammed the ground and ricocheted away with shrill, deadly whines.

The hole was hardly deep enough to hide him. A chunk of lead creased his back. Another showered him with dirt when it hit close on the rim of the hollow.

Russ realized the first bullet had come from the right where Caloon should have been. Was his partner warning him? The rain of lead stopped and Russ eased up to check on his comrade.

Caloon was bolting for the woods at an amazing speed. His hat sailed away from his head. From behind the man a fusillade of rifle fire roared. Russ saw Caloon miss a step, then fold and strike the earth. He was up fast. Limping badly, he struggled for the juniper only a few feet away.

A shot struck Caloon. Russ saw him jerk under the impact. He nearly fell, but caught himself and staggered forward. Almost simultaneously two chunks of lead tore him to the ground.

On the slope near the camp, Raasleer listened to the rifle shots from two different locations. He turned with a satisfied smile to the five men sitting their ponies near him. "Corddry and the others have killed them. Now we'll go do our job."

The outlaws spurred noisily down the rocky grade toward the Palomas Desert, and beyond that, the Growler Mountains.

Russ peered through the grass growing on the lip of the hollow. His enemies were squatting on the fringe of the evergreens and speedily reloading their weapons. He rotated his view to discover the location of Caloon's killers. He found them at a range twice as long and also cramming shells into their rifles.

Never again would all four guns be empty at the exact time. Russ sucked in a lung full of air, sprang from the hole, and dashed for the nearest juniper. Every ounce of his strength went into his churning legs, his reaching feet. His eyes were riveted on that tree. Could he run with two slugs in him, if he had to, like Caloon?

A second stretched endlessly. The juniper came closer so very slowly. He never heard the shot, but the bullet whizzed past in front of his face. A second plucked at his leg.

Run! Run! The green woods were less than a room's width away. Then he plunged into them. He continued to run for an additional fifty yards, halted abruptly, and turned straight for his enemies.

They had killed Caloon without giving him a chance. Could they also kill him? The four of them could if he did not ambush them. They deserved to be shot in the back.

A juniper, perhaps twice the height of a man and quite broad, grew by itself in a small clearing. It had many limbs, densely covered with needles. The thick foliage extended from the ground to the very topmost crown of the tree.

Russ parted the long tree limbs and pushed deeply into them, until he was pressed tightly to the trunk of the tree, completely hidden. He waited, perfectly motionless and facing in the direction from which he had come.

A minute passed. A second, then three. His breathing was slow now and silent.

On the opposite side of the tree, a twig snapped. A barely audible scuff of a foot came from his right. Two men came around the juniper and stopped, not twenty feet away.

Russ raised his arm, parted the branches noiselessly, and aimed his six-gun at the nearest man. "Corddry," he whispered.

The man whirled. Russ shot his heart out.

Instantly he shifted his gun to Kanttner and killed him before he could point his weapon.

Russ rested his arm on a limb and stilled the tremor that was trying to start. What a terrible way to kill men. Giving them no chance. He clinched his teeth—just like they had killed Caloon.

He waited. Have patience, he cautioned himself. They heard the shots and will come.

Nothing moved. There was absolutely no sound. He seriously considered taking one of the rifles and going after the two remaining men. Each time the idea tempted him, he fought it back.

Time passed. A breeze stirred the top of the juniper. He could make out Corddry's feet through a small opening in the foliage.

A man's whisper startled Russ. "Damnation. They're both dead."

Russ shifted his head ever so slightly. Dazell stood beside the bodies. His vigilant eyes were sweeping the trees all around. Jones crouched near him, his rifle poised.

"Both shot," Dazell whispered again. "Look, they're laying right together. Killed without them getting off a shot. How could that be?"

Russ saw Dazell look at the dead men, evaluating the wounds. Then the man turned to directly face his hiding place.

"In the tree!" Dazell screamed and with lightning speed brought up his rifle.

Russ shot Dazell in the center of the chest. Jones fired into the tree, missing. Russ returned the shot and saw Jones collapse.

Russ pushed out of the enclosing branches of the juniper. He wasted no time on the men. Let the buzzards pick their bones. With hasty steps, he went to his friend. The man had given his life to warn him.

Caloon lay on his face. Gently Russ turned him over.

The man's eyes opened slowly, heavily. "All dead?" he asked, his voice a murmur that Russ, in great surprise, strained to hear.

"All dead, you tough old bastard," said Russ huskily, his eyes growing moist. "You saved my life."

"Always was a little crazy at times," whispered Caloon. He coughed and the pain blanked out his eyes for a moment.

Russ saw the gaping wounds in the man, the blood in great pools on the ground, and did not know how he continued to live.

As if answering Russ's silent question, Caloon whispered again. "I couldn't die until I knew if you were alive."

He tried to raise his hand to touch his young friend, but could not make the hand move. "It's good to die with a friend near." The whisper trailed away to a soft exhaling of air. Then even that ended.

Chapter 18

Beneath the vast bowl of the pale blue sky, the big sorrel ran easily, swinging his powerful legs, devouring mile after mile of the cactus-and-brush-studded Palomas Desert. Russ rode effortlessly, his body meshed with the rhythm of the mustang's stride. A second horse, a tall gray on a long lead rope, trailed behind.

After Caloon's death, Russ scouted the camp for other members of the gang. It was empty with many tracks heading down into the desert.

Russ sighted along the course, and saw the six outlaws had set a beeline for the Growler Mountains in the far distance. He knew what their intentions were, and, further, that Raasleer had a five- or six-mile head start. A great fear arose in him that the killers would reach the girl and her family before he could arrive and help them.

He hurriedly caught Caloon's two horses and threw a saddle upon one. He left at once, hounding the trail of the rustlers. That had been twenty miles behind.

At the bank of the Gila River, Russ pulled the horses down to a walk. The river was shallow and they waded across and entered the Sentinel Desert. He let the ponies walk for another half mile then touched the one he rode with spurs and pushed him into a canter.

Two hours later he changed the saddle to the second horse and turned the first animal, blown and lathered with sweat, loose to fend for himself. Russ was weary; he had ridden fifty miles since daylight. Yet a few miles later, when his mount began to falter in its ascent of the steep west flank of the Growler, he stepped down and finished climbing the mountain on foot.

Russ reached the top and remounted. When he came out of the confining walls of the pass, he heard faint gunshots at the base of the mountain. They continued sporadically. The Tamblins were still alive, or at least one was. Russ began a rapid descent, crowding the horse recklessly down the east face.

He checked the sun. There was an hour of daylight, then an hour of dusk before the darkness. With the darkness would come death to the Tamblins.

In the upper end of Growler Valley, the Englishman found tracks of several horses coming from the northwest. He discussed the discovery with Prim Herrera and Shallow. Herrera, after hiding for a day and resting from his gunshot wound, had made his way to Edmonton's camp to inform him of his relative's death and the rustler gang's departure. Disappointed by the ease with which Raasleer had slipped past them, the rancher had struck out for home.

Now evaluating the sign on the ground, Edmonton realized the outlaws would have had time to return to their hideout and be off on another raid on some unsuspecting rancher's cattle. Except this time I am only an hour behind you with twelve good men on strong horses, and there is no storm in the sky to hide you.

"Let's go!" he cried to his men. "This time we shall not fail."

Like a pack of aroused hunting dogs they eagerly took to the trail.

Russ warily approached the head of the valley that contained the cabin and spring. He rode the low swales and used every bit of cover offered by the sparse, waist-high brush on the mountainside. No shots had sounded for some time.

When close enough to discern details, he stopped on a bluff a few hundred feet above the spring to reconnoiter. How was the fight going? Where was the enemy?

The telescope came out and began to scan the land below. He saw a man with ten or twelve horses hidden in a hollow down the creek from the cabin.

A rifle cracked from the brush and rock to the right of the house. A quick shot answered from a window on that side. The Tamblins were still able to fight.

Russ now had two members of the gang located. The others were hidden there someplace on the hillside, waiting for the defenders to make a mistake and expose themselves to their guns, or for night to fall and cover their frontal attack upon the cabin.

The sun was sinking rapidly and bringing long shadows into the valley. A lone hawk flew up from the desert, heading for its nighttime perch on the high crags of the mountain. He saw the humans below and veered off abruptly to go around.

Russ tied his horse and moved to the opposite end of the bluff in preparation to slip closer to the battleground and take a hand in the fighting. A sharp bird whistle floated down from the ridge above him. Russ hunched low and, concentrating on the valley, did not turn to look.

The whistle sounded again, more imperative. He tossed a

glance in that direction. The skinny old Indian called Raven, holding a rifle in the crook of his arm, stood looking at him. His hand came up in greeting.

In deep surprise, Russ raised his hand and returned the salute. Surely the Apaches were not the ones attacking the Tamblins. The track of Raasleer's gang had led directly to this location.

Raven whistled again—a different call—and a few seconds later Rock That Rolls and Sun Wolf glided in smoothly to stand near him. Silent as shadows, they came down the slope toward Russ.

All the warriors seated themselves. Russ squatted facing them. He looked at the wound on the young brave. Like a young, wild animal, the Indian boy-man was healing quickly and thoroughly.

The Indian touched his old injury, prodded it to show there was no pain. Russ nodded his understanding.

The third Indian was the big warrior who had threatened Russ with the rifle in the rainstorm, days past. He was only slightly more friendly now. As Russ waited for the Indians to explain their presence here, three more warriors catfooted in quietly from the brush.

Raven asked in a hushed voice, "Which are your people?"

"The ones in the cabin," answered Russ, also keeping his voice low. "Why are you here?"

"We plan to take what is left after the battle is over," said Raven.

"The men in the rocks are outlaws, killers. They are the ones that did that." Russ pointed to the wound on Rock That Rolls. "But the people in the house are my friends. I ask you not to harm them."

"We owe you nothing," said Sun Wolf, his tone unfriendly.

"That is correct," agreed Russ. "But are the Apaches

eagles who take what they want, or are they buzzards that eat the carrion after stronger men fight?"

Sun Wolf's face became ferocious and he started to raise his rifle. Even Raven showed anger, but he controlled it and said, "We have only a handful of warriors now because we fought like the eagle, and we died bravely like the eagle. From now on we must be more cunning and less seen than the fox if we are to continue as a people."

Russ recognized the wisdom in Raven's words. "My tongue is not that of a friend and my mind is dull," said Russ in apology. "Your people need horses and guns and gold to buy other things. Will you help me kill all the men in the rocks for two thousand dollars in gold and many strong mustangs?" He felt confident that among all the outlaws there would be two thousand dollars.

Sun Wolf shook his head. "We will have all those things and much more by the time the sun comes up *mañana*."

"If you do what I ask, you will have friends who may be of great help to you someday."

The Ancient One removed his view from the white man and looked at the faces of his people. Except for Sun Wolf and himself, they were all young. Their fathers and uncles were now dust. White friends might help these last members of his tribe survive; perhaps there was no other way they could survive. "How can we slay them without many of us also dying?"

"I will call their chief out and fight him," said Russ. "While his men are watching, you slip upon them and destroy them with those." He pointed to the rifles the braves carried.

The Indians talked among themselves in their own language. Raven spoke at length to them.

Finally Sun Wolf turned to Russ. "The Ancient One has again convinced me to help you."

"There are six of my enemies," said Russ. "Do you know where all are hidden?"

"Yes, we know," said Sun Wolf. "Which one will you fight?"

"He is a very tall man, thin like the saguaro cactus. Do you know where he is?"

Sun Wolf motioned Russ to follow. They crawled to where they could look down onto the cabin and the surrounding valley and hillsides.

"The man you talk about is there on the other side in the rocks." He pointed.

"Good. How much time will you need to get your warriors ready?"

"We want none of them to escape, so I will kill the man with their mustangs first. After that is done, I will signal from there with this." He touched the dirty white cotton shirt he wore. "Only you from up here will be able to see me. Then, while you hold the eyes of the other enemies, my people will slay them."

Sun Wolf left silently, collecting the others behind him. Russ never once saw them as they stole across the hillside to take up positions against their prey.

After a few minutes, Sun Wolf's white shirt flashed from the hollow where the horses were. Russ knew one rustler was dead. Would the next man to die be himself?

Staying concealed in the brush, Russ called out loudly. "Raasleer, do you hear me?"

Complete silence held in the valley.

"Raasleer, you cowardly bastard, do you hear me?" cried Russ at the top of his lungs, wanting all the outlaws to hear.

"I hear you," responded Raasleer angrily, his voice booming. "What do you want?"

"You dead. I'm going to kill you."

Raasleer's laugh came rolling over the hillside. "Where's your crazy sidekick?"

"He's dead, murdered by your back-shooting gang. Are you a back shooter too, Raasleer, or will you face me man to man?" taunted Russ.

"Where's Corddry and the others?" called Raasleer.

"Dead. Same as my partner. Are you going to stand up and show all your men how fast you are with a six-gun?"

"I should've killed you long ago," said Raasleer savagely. "Come on down and make your stand."

"We come out in the open at the same time," responded Russ. "Tell your men not to shoot."

"Hold your fire," called Raasleer loudly, confidently. "All of you hold your fire. I'll take care of this. Won't take but a minute. All right, kid. I'll meet you down the draw around that first bend. I don't want the rancher to shoot me after I blast you."

"I agree," said Russ. Very carefully he checked his six-gun. Then he crouched down below the tops of the brush and worked across the grade of the hill.

Just downstream from where the channel curved stiffly to the right, the slopes of the hill retreated back and allowed the bottom to double in width to nearly two hundred yards. At the edge of the flat, Russ hesitated in a clump of brush and scanned the area selected by Raasleer for the shoot-out. The flat was without brush. The cabin was out of sight, upstream some five hundred feet. Just downstream from him, the irrigated meadow began. The water from the spring flowed in a rocky bed in the center of the valley bottom straight in front of him.

Raasleer moved out of the protective cover of the desert brush and into the open. Russ stood up straight and stepped onto the floor of the valley to meet him.

For a short moment, Russ stopped and gazed up at the sky. He breathed deeply, then exhaled slowly. The most dangerous challenge of his life was just seconds away. He had seen Raasleer draw and shoot with unbelievable swiftness and accuracy. Had he made a mistake in challenging him?

Russ dropped his view to the rustler chief. The man

walked steadily, drawing closer, yet at too long a distance for pistols. Russ strode forward to confront him.

The space between the two men narrowed to fifty yards, then less. Get ready, Raven, thought Russ, you and your people must kill the outlaws even if I lose the fight. Pretty Girl Tamblin, I hope you have a long and happy life.

Russ could make out Raasleer's face now, but it was devoid of life, as noncommittal as a rock. There would be no telltale expression there to show when he was going to draw his weapon.

They stopped as of one accord, each staring directly into the other's face. Except for the uncaring water of the brook making its liquid noises on the rocks at their feet, the valley was perfectly silent.

Why wait for Raasleer? thought Russ. Why give him the edge of starting first? Russ brought his hand up, fingering his six-gun from its holster.

Raasleer, the expert gunman, read the young man's decision before it was fully made. His hand blurred, coming up with his pistol. Flame lanced out at his enemy.

Russ's gun was already bucking in his hand, the bullet slugging Raasleer in the chest, knocking his shot partially off mark. Russ felt a blow on his left side. He fired again, into the heart of his opponent.

Raasleer staggered. His face twisted with surprise, then went blank. He fell backward heavily.

In the rocks on the hillside, a volley of shots crashed. Followed a moment later by the piercing victory cry of an Apache warrior. Russ thought he recognized the voice of the old Indian, Raven.

Russ began to hurt. He ran his fingers over the side of his rib cage beneath his left arm. Raasleer's slug had been boring for his lungs, but it had been off target and the heavy chest bones had deflected it. The speeding slug had torn a deep groove in the flesh, extending from front to back.

Russ pressed his arm tightly against his side, trying to slow the flow of blood that poured out hot and wet.

The Indians, no longer trying to stay hidden, became visible angling up across the mountainside. Sun Wolf, riding one of the rustler's horses and leading the remainder, hastened to catch the rest of the warriors. As he overtook a brave, the man would swing astride one of the ponies. Soon all were mounted and moving swiftly, disappeared from sight.

Russ heard footsteps coming close. He turned, holding his six-gun ready. The older Tamblin trotted toward him. Behind him a few paces came the girl and the third Tamblin. All carried rifles.

"You all right?" asked Lafe, seeing the crimson stain working its way down Russ's side.

"Got nicked somewhat," said Russ and holstered his gun.

"Damn good work. You sure shot hell out of that *hombre*. So that's Raasleer. Doesn't look like much dead."

"Not much of a looker alive either," said Russ, grimacing as the pain built up.

"Probably not. I hope your Indian friends killed all the other bushwhackers in the rocks," said Lafe.

"I'm certain they did."

"Oh, stop talking," interjected Samantha. "Can't you see he's hurt and needs help?" She walked up very close and tenderly took hold of his arm on the wounded side.

Russ gazed deeply into her eyes. She had touched him. Dare he touch her? He put out his hand and brushed her cheeks with his fingertips, enjoying the contact, the feel of the perfect smoothness of her skin.

The color came rushing into her face and he took his hand away.

"The Indians are coming back," said Dan Tamblin in a warning voice.

With a rumble of hooves on the hard ground, the warriors rode up to stop near Russ and the Tamblins. The braves had shifted to their own ponies and now led the rustlers' mounts.

Raven looked down at Raasleer's body and then at Russ. "You would make a good Apache warrior," he said.

Sun Wolf pulled a leather pouch from his belt. "Found more gold than the two thousand dollars. Here." He tossed the bag to Russ.

Russ caught it. "You keep it," he said and reached up to offer it back.

"No," said Sun Wolf firmly. "The price was agreed on."

One of the braves called out sharply in his own language. All the Indians turned to look up the mountain toward the pass.

Raven twisted back to look at Russ. "Many men on ponies coming. We must go now."

"I wish you long lives, *amigos,*" said Russ. He put his hand up in farewell.

"A long life," repeated Raven. There was a wistful look behind his eyes. He raised his hand, palm out, toward Russ.

Sun Wolf spoke to his mustang and the animal bolted away at a full run. The other warriors thundered after him, dragging the captured horses.

"The bleeding needs to be stopped," said Lafe. He moved up and tore Russ's shirt open to expose the wound. "Not all that bad. I bet it smarts some and it's bleeding fairly heavy. But we can stop that. Long as it doesn't get infected, you'll be good as new in a week or two."

"Grandfather, do you think these men that are coming will hurt him?" asked Samantha.

"Well, are they after you?" questioned Lafe, his eyes intently probing Russ's face.

"Too late to worry about that now," said Dan Tamblin. "Here they come."

Edmonton and his cowboys pulled to a halt close to the group. "We heard the shooting and came fast as we could. You're the Tamblins, aren't you? Everybody all right?"

"Yes, we're the Tamblins," said Dan. "Raasleer's been killed by this young fellow. And his gang of rustlers are dead up on the hillside."

Shallow wheeled his horse to ride up and stare down at the corpse near the creek. He turned and nodded to Edmonton. "This *hombre* fits what I've been told Raasleer looked like."

"Who were those riders I saw leaving in such a rush?" asked Edmonton.

"Friends of ours," said Lafe.

"I see," said Edmonton, evaluating the girl and the strained face of the young man standing tensely and alertly beside her.

Edmonton questioned Russ. "What's your name?"

"Russ Tarlow." He read the suspicious look on the rancher's face. Cattle rustlers were hung in the Arizona Territory.

"He's one of us," interrupted Lafe in a tight voice and stepped up to stand near Russ. "If it hadn't been for him calling Raasleer out and killing him, we would all be dead by now."

"So he is one of you," said the Englishman. He whirled to look at Prim Herrera. "Do you know this man?"

His arm in a sling, Herrera guided his horse up close to Russ. For a long moment he stared down into Russ's face. "He is a stranger, Señor Edmonton."

"So that's the way it's going to be," said the Englishman.

Russ tugged the pouch of gold Sun Wolf had given him from his pocket. He extracted a second bag containing his and Caloon's gold, for he had taken his friend's valuables, and handed them up to the Englishman. "This gold was found on the rustlers. Maybe you can find the rightful owners."

Edmonton hefted the gold in his hand. His eyes were softer. "What do you plan to do now?"

Russ considered that question. The range of possibilities for his future was changing rapidly. He glanced at Samantha. "I'm going to start a ranch on the Kofas," he answered.

"Well, then you'll need some money to buy breeding stock. Here, take this as a loan." He pitched the precious metal to Russ.

"I may not be able to repay you for a long time," exclaimed Russ, amazed at his sudden turn of fortune.

"Just keep rustlers out of the Kofas," replied Edmonton in a stern voice, "that'll be payment enough."

"There'll never be another rustler in those mountains," promised Russ. "I might find some stolen cows over that way. When I do I'll return them to their rightful owners."

"Your word's good enough for me," said Edmonton. "I'll be over to visit you from time to time and help you with any cattle you find."

He turned to his men. "Come on, you cowboys. Let's see how far toward home we can ride before it gets dark." He smiled at Samantha and loped his horse down the valley.

"Let's take Russ to the cabin, so we can stop his bleeding," said Samantha. "Please hurry."

As Russ started to move with the girl, the weakness from his injury caused him to stagger. Lafe and Dan saw his distress and stepped in quickly to catch him.

The strong hands helped Russ to walk. He thought of what Caloon had said. "It's good to die with a friend near."

Well, old friend, it is even better to be alive and near friends.

Samantha heard Russ laugh. She was worried about his wound, yet she felt happy. She took his hand and smiled.

About the Author

F. M. Parker has worked as a sheepherder, lumberman, sailor, factory worker, geologist, and a manager of wild horses, buffalo, and livestock grazing. He currently manages several thousand acres of rangeland in eastern Oregon.